Praise for Black Days, Bloody Nights

"*Black Days and Bloody Nights* delivers on its title with clear intent and dark creativity. Greg Chapman's latest collection is bleak, horrific and utterly compulsive, spanning tales of religious fanaticism, possession, psychological torment, and the end of days. Often emotionally anchored in family dynamics, the stories are hellish whirlpools, sucking you into the grim, visceral world of Chapman's imagination and holding you captive until each devastating maelstrom has played out. Black days and bloody nights, indeed."
—Geneve Flynn, two-time Bram Stoker and Shirley Jackson Award winner

"*Black Days and Bloody Nights* is a powerhouse collection of bleak horror stories full of religious zealots, psychological torment, and demonic forces. Read it, then find someone to hold you tight as you cry for all of humanity."
—Zac Ashford, Aurealis Award-nominated author of *The Morass* and *Polyphemus*

"Rife with terror, tension and torment from the first story to the last, this collection shows the gifted Chapman at the top of his game."
—Kaaron Warren, Shirley Jackson Award-winning author of *Sky* and *The Grief Hole*

"Greg Chapman's work not only combines vivid description with three dimensional characters you invest in, his stories make you think. Just the kind of horror I can get behind."
—Paul Kane, #1 bestselling, award-winning author of *Sherlock Holmes and the Servants of Hell*, *Before* and *The Gemini Effect*

"Dark fiction that'll have you riveted."
—Steve Stred, author of *Churn the Soil*

T0340853

GREG CHAPMAN'S BOOKS PUBLISHED BY IFWG

Midnight Masquerade (2023)
Black Days and Bloody Nights (2024)

BLACK DAYS AND BLOODY NIGHTS

BY GREG CHAPMAN

IFWG Publishing Australia
Gold Coast
www.ifwgaustralia.com

TABLE OF CONTENTS

FOREWORD

BY STEVE STRED

Horror fiction is an interesting beast, isn't it?

Every day, on every social media platform, you'll see people posting in search of specific subgenres of horror that they want to read.

The reality of it is there are simply too many subgenres to even list.

But, we can offer a generalization that no matter the subgenre, reading horror fiction is, at its base, an escape. An escape from real life: work, family, bills, politics, the weather, finances, it goes on and on. Each reader who picks up something to read is entering a world new to them and one that will take them away from whatever it is that they're dealing with at the moment.

What a wonderful thing.

Now, some may call me odd with what I'm about to say but, much like the music I enjoy, when I pick up something to read, I tend to gravitate more towards the stories that crush my soul. The ones that cause my breath to hitch, my eyes to well up and my subconscious to ask me just what in the hell I was thinking.

Horror fiction is that rare breed that allows a writer to simultaneously scare the pants off the reader, while also making them reach for the Kleenex box as characters they've grown to love struggle through a horrible situation and, far too often, don't survive.

It's this penchant for my enjoyment of dark fiction that makes me despondent and filled with sorrow that led me to the author whose book you hold in your hands.

When I was a member of the Kendall Reviews team, I snagged the novella, *The Followers* by Greg Chapman. I'd not read anything by Greg up to that point and was excited to see just what it entailed. I was stunned. Originally titled *The Eschatologist,* this post-apocalyptic story had me hooked and I wondered why more people weren't raving about it. What truly had me enamored was the atmosphere. This dense, layered, seething sense of hopelessness practically screamed off the page. I was hooked. Greg Chapman had me. It's a funny thing when you find an author whose work you admire so much. Thanks to the internet, we can immediately fire up Google or Amazon or Goodreads and search out their work. In this case, what did I find? Chapman was a Bram Stoker-nominated author. That he had a bunch of work out already. AND! And he was a talented cover designer and illustrator.

WHAT?!

When *Netherkind* was released in 2019, I devoured it. It is still one of my all-time favorite novels. And once again, Greg packed it to the brim with sorrow-tinged atmosphere and an underlying feeling of hopelessness. It was around this time that I somehow managed to get on Greg's radar and he reached out directly to me when new releases were on the horizon. I never once hesitated to accept and in one case, the collection he sent me was so friggin' good, I believe I read it that night in a single sitting. All the while, Greg's prose kept me coming back, kept me hooked and ready to bawl like a baby.

That collection was *This Sublime Darkness And Other Dark Stories.* It destroyed me. Go read it.

Vaudeville and Other Nightmares destroyed me. Go read it. Hell, the title story alone is one of the best novellas I've ever read, but we can't forget the story "The Only Son." Even thinking back about this story has me on the cusp of needing to wipe my eyes dry. (And I'm not even mentioning "Deluge," a story just as good as both of those.)

And, while I'm waxing about Chapman's desire to decimate his readers, don't forget about his debut novel, *Hollow House,* which is essentially a cry-fest masquerading as a horror story.

Which brings us around to *Black Days and Bloody Nights.*

To say I was humbled and over the moon when Greg emailed me about writing a foreword to this collection is an understatement. Greg and I have developed a great relationship over the years, which has also led to Greg doing some cover work for me. If you're looking for a cover artist, seriously consider Greg. His artwork is stunning and he's one of the easiest-going folks to work with.

But I digress. Just what awaits you after you've finished this foreword and flipped the page?

Dark fiction that'll have you riveted. Stories that will have you rooting for someone only to have your heart ripped from your chest. Pieces that'll make you think long and hard about just how you'd handle that situation, were you to find yourself in it.

I'm personally not a fan of forewords that go into great detail about each story you're about to read. It can feel like you're watching a preview for the movie that is about to play. Saying that, I want to introduce a few of them. I want the excitement of what you're about to experience to start now.

This one opens with the previously-mentioned *The Followers*, and honestly, that sets the stage for the rest of the collection. A post-apocalyptic survival story that showcases Greg's phenomenal way of creating characters and filling the page with dread. He follows that up with the title story, about a mysterious eclipse and an infected man. "Black Days and Bloody Nights" is poised to be a fan favorite, if not one to make the leap to a cinematic adaptation. "The Five Stages of Grief" and "Like Father, Like Son" both touch on similar topics, dealing with loss, grief and difficult parental decisions, and "Don't Watch" makes you do the exact opposite, in a story surrounding a mysterious tape.

"The Yellow House" (Oh, hello Carcosa and the Yellow King) and "Torment" bring us to the very end.

There's a few stories I've purposely left out, wanting to try and keep some of the element of surprise for you, but trust me when I say, you won't be disappointed.

Black Days and Bloody Nights shows the many ways Greg Chapman controls the reader from start to finish and delivers stories that absolutely punish the reader. From fright to sorrow and everything in between, Greg's writing showcases how a talented author can work within a number of subgenres and simply (and easily) make them his own.

A modern master craftsman, Greg is an author that should be on every reader's TBRs. He should also be one that is a "must-buy" author and one that goes right to the top of the pile.

I know he is for me.

I think I'll close it there.

Actually, two last things, while I have you.

First off, do yourself a favor and buy another of his books right now. No, seriously, go. I'll wait. There we go, thanks for that. Welcome back. You've just made a smart decision, because when you've finished this one, you'll be kicking yourself if you didn't have another of Greg's books waiting for you to dive right into.

Secondly, once you begin to read this—and I'm 100% sure this will happen—don't be afraid to tell everyone about this. *The Followers* kicks off with a bang, and when that hits, go to Twitter, go to Facebook or Instagram or Mastodon or Hive or TikTok and tell everyone that you're reading this collection. And when you finish this collection—and before you start that other Chapman book you ordered—make sure you leave a review. Amazon, Goodreads, Bookbub, wherever. Even a few words helps each and every author, and some authors don't like asking for them, so in this case, I'll ask for Greg.

I do hope you love this collection as much as I did.

You're in steady hands and a warped brain and I couldn't be happier for you.

Steve Stred
February 3rd, 2023
Edmonton, Alberta, Canada

THE FOLLOWERS

The afterworld was a canvas of ashen ruin painted by death.

Such thoughts should not have entered the heart of Father Malcolm Forde, but how could he deny what he saw before him?

The horizon stretched in an endless line of turquoise cloud, the landscape devoid of any structure apart from craggy rocks ejected from the earth. Father Forde walked, stirring up more dust with each footfall. He pressed the flimsy breathing mask tight over his face, wishing there was something he could put over his eyes.

No, I must not think like this; there is always hope.

He pulled his fraying coat tighter and let his gaze drift to the red earth beneath his shoes. He mouthed a prayer to his Lord God, a silent affirmation of his faith.

Lead me to green pastures. Lead me to your flock. The ones you have spared this…this…

His prayer caught in his throat and became a hacking cough. He bent at the waist and heaved. Vomit flooded his throat, and he quickly pulled the face mask aside to let it splatter on the ground. Blood mingled with the meager scraps of canned meat he'd eaten just hours before, when he had come across an abandoned house. The blood was God's response, he thought to himself, that he wasn't worthy of saving.

Hands trembling, Father Forde reached inside his satchel and retrieved a water can. A trickle ran into his mouth and down his beard to soak into his once white priest's collar. The fluid quenched the fire in his throat. After catching his breath, he looked to sky with pleading eyes.

Is this how Your Son felt at Gethsemane?

The priest wiped his mouth and squinted at the hell all around him. How had it come to this? Man had turned its eye from God, become swollen on self-worth and fortune, and eventually, the Devil had had his due. The earthquakes and storms came and the Garden of Eden was left torn and barren. The few who believed were left to labor in the waste, to wander aimlessly in the vain hope that faith would deliver them through.

No, no, there is purpose in this. He always has a purpose for us.

Tears welled in his eyes as his body betrayed his heart. He wiped them away, those tears of shame, and his vision became clearer. In the distance he glimpsed a figure, one of God's own children, walking towards him.

Father Forde stood and stared at the impossible sight. He prayed that it wasn't a trick of the eye. The gritty, hot wind buffeted the figure as it approached, its ratty hooded cloak slapping the air. The man of God was frozen in awe as the figure came closer and closer. Not rushing, simply walking, a lone survivor just like him.

Perhaps there is hope after all?

All too briefly, the blanket of decrepit cloud parted, and a shaft of sunlight painted the figure in gold. The priest blinked and saw the stranger standing before him, a man, much younger than he, his face obscured by the hood and thickening stubble.

"Praise God," Father Forde said, lifting his hand in a bid to see if the man was tangible. His new companion took a step back. "It's so good to see you."

The stranger remained at a distance, so the priest bent to try and see under his hood.

"What's your name, son?"

He failed—or refused—to respond. The wind howled around them.

"Are you hurt? Can you speak?" said the priest. "My name is Forde, Malcolm Forde. Father Malcolm Forde."

The cloak fluttered and snapped. Forde stepped closer, desperate to see the man's eyes, to make contact with this living soul.

"Are you hungry?" He turned to his satchel and pulled out

the opened can of SPAM. "I'd be most grateful for you to share it with me. It's been so long since I've seen anyone. I kind of wish I had stayed in the west, but I felt God's call. 'Go out and find my children,' He said."

Forde chuckled, trying to break the ice. The man was a statue. "Please, son, won't you tell me your name?"

Cracked lips parted beneath the hood. "Pray."

The dry voice was caught by the wind.

"What did you say?" Forde asked, leaning closer.

There was a rustling as the man opened his cloak and produced a well-worn Bible. The leather cover was split at the corners, the gilded edges of the pages dulled and flecked. Forde noticed the man's hands were unwashed, with black muck beneath his fingernails.

"Oh, you want to pray?" the priest said, smiling at his own complacency. "Of course, of course—just let me get mine—"

The man pushed his Bible into the priest's hand. "Pray."

"Oh, yes, forgive me," Forde said. "The Word is the Word."

The thin pages curled in the breeze as he opened the man's Bible. The interior was as filthy as his hands. As he flicked through for an appropriate passage, he saw the man drop to his knees and clasp his hands in preparedness.

This man is truly devout. Is he my answer? Has God sent me a companion for these dark times?

"Pray," the stranger said once more.

Forde felt the man's urgency pervade him and he quickly turned to Paul's Letter to the Ephesians.

"Let us pray. 'For this reason, I fall on my knees to the Father, from whom every family in heaven and on earth receives its true name. I ask God from the wealth of his glory to give you power through his Spirit to be strong in your inner selves, and I pray that Christ will make his home in your hearts through faith—"

"Stop," the man said.

Forde looked down for a better view of the man's face. The skin was almost white, but cracked and peeling. Flecks of dried blood were spattered about the nose and jaw, but it was the shadow over the man's eyes which pulled Forde in, a shadow cold and deep that not even the glaring sun seemed able to penetrate.

"Is there something wrong?"

The man never blinked. "Shouldn't we be reading from Revelations?"

Forde looked down at the words of Saint Paul, as if they could help him. "I'm sorry?"

"These are the end times. The words of Saint John are all that matter now."

Forde turned the pages back, his old heart suddenly pounding out a warning.

"The Gospel; yes, the words of Christ are more—"

A grubby hand reached up to grab the book. "No." The man stood and wrenched the Bible from Forde's grasp. The trembling priest watched as the man pulled the tasseled bookmark to flip to the back of the tome. "The Book of Revelations is at the back. You should know that, Father." He handed it back to Forde, and the priest glared at the opening page, the words of Saint John, splattered with old blood. "Read," the man ordered.

Father Forde's throat clicked with dryness. He swallowed and took a tremulous breath before reading the words of Saint John.

"'Then I saw the Lamb break open the first of the seven seals, and I heard one of the four living creatures say in a voice that sounded like thunder, "Come!" I looked, and there was a white horse. Its rider held a bow, and he was given a crown. He rode out as a conqueror to conquer—"

From his cloak the stranger revealed a long, wide-bladed knife. Its edge glimmered with some inner light.

"Do you not remember me, Father?" the stranger said.

Forde looked up from Saint John's Revelations, but he could only stare at the knife. "No, son, I don't know you… Should I?"

The hooded man shifted the knife from his left hand to his right. The priest flinched.

"I remember you," the man said. "God sent me to find you. I admit I had my doubts, just like Thomas, but here you are standing before me."

Father Forde gently closed the Bible and tried to hand it back to him.

"I'm sorry, son, but I can't stay," Forde said, his terrified heart shaking his voice. "I must move on and find others to minister to."

The stranger lowered his arms to his sides. "Am I not worth ministering to, Father? Do I not have faith? Have I not carried my faith all my life—even when you sought to hurt me?"

Forde stepped to the side and made to walk past the stranger. "Forgive me, son, but I know not what you mean. Perhaps it's best that we part ways here."

"Forgive you?" The stranger smiled and laughed, but it was little more than a shrug. "God could never forgive you for what you've done in His name." The man peeled back his hood, revealing the characteristic pale pink complexion of an albino. Forde no longer fixated on the knife; instead, he was drawn to the man's pearlescent, darting eyes. God help him, Father Forde knew those eyes.

"Oh my God, you—"

The stranger replaced his hood. "God has named me His apostle, His prophet for these end times—Amos—and with His blessing, all sinners will face His judgement."

Forde opened his mouth to plead for his life, but with a backhanded swipe, Amos gave the priest a new mouth from which to preach. From those lips spilled the first blood of God's new covenant with the last of mankind.

1

David Brewer stared at the revolver in his hand. He ran shaking fingers over its dull metal surface, traced the curve of the barrel, the notches in the handgrip. David knew the gun all too well; it had been a constant reminder of the moment before everything in his life had lost its worth. It made sense that it should be the gun he would use to kill himself and his family.

He looked up from the gun and out into the wasteland. The few trees, dark and decayed, appeared as if they would turn to dust in the slightest breeze. The entire world was dust, held together by a promise that would never be fulfilled. Ashes to ashes, dust to dust. There was no God to pray to here. The only god David believed in was Death.

David snapped open the chamber of the revolver, counted the six bullets nestled inside, and closed it again. He turned away from the scene to consider his wife and daughter curled up together, sleeping beside the smoking remnants of the previous night's fire.

Six bullets; there'd be three left after. *Maybe someone might find you. They'd have a gun with three bullets then.*

David slipped the revolver deep inside the pocket of his torn coat and wiped tears from his eyes as another thought crossed his mind.

Maybe it would just be easier if you only used one bullet? Then Marci and Kaley would have five left to protect themselves. Wouldn't that be a greater mercy?

His wife rolled over and opened her eyes to look at him. Immediately, David saw the fear settle in her gaze. He hated seeing that look in her, that desperate need.

Marci pulled back the blanket and walked to him, wrapping her arms vice-like around his waist. "Why didn't you wake me?"

"I thought you could use some more sleep," he lied. David pulled himself from her embrace and kept his eyes on the dead trees sprouting between the hills of shattered rock. He couldn't stand the sight of her, her smell—or his own. It made him sick. They smelled of the world around them: the slow stink of rot.

Marci approached again, and David started to walk into the woods.

"Where are you going?" she said with that shrill of worry in her voice.

"To find breakfast. Wake Kaley and get her to start collecting wood for a fire."

David picked up his pace, grateful the crunch of rotten tree branches and rubble underfoot drowned out his wife's pleas. As he walked away, he slipped his fingers around his cold, familiar friend.

Soon, the voice told him. *Soon.*

David plunged his hands into the freezing stream and flinched. The cold crawled up his arms, wormlike fingers stabbing their way to his heart. If anything, the sensation was a distraction, a different feeling than despair, fear and self-loathing. Any feeling would do. When the water began to burn, he pulled his hands free and rubbed them over his face. He took off his cap and raked wet fingers through his hair and down the back of his neck, trying to dispel the fear.

Just kill yourself.

He thought of the gun. It, too, was a welcome cold. He could put it in his mouth, pull the trigger, and leave this sorry world behind.

If you weren't such a fucking coward.

The thought slapped him harder than the icy stream, and he retrieved the gun. He felt its weight.

Go on, use it!

The rims of the six bullets were like judging eyes. He should have grabbed the automatic, he told himself. But it was impossible to think straight when your world was literally tearing itself down before your eyes, and your family is looking to you to save them.

You've spent years helping others, walking the beat. Maybe it's time to help yourself?

David ignored the mental jibe and took a deep breath. The woods seemed to close in on him, the trickle of the stream rising to a roar. He stood, shaking his head in a bid to push the thoughts from his mind.

"I'm fucking losing it," he said.

He slapped himself in the face. The ugly little voice was getting louder; he had to keep it on a leash. Had he actually contemplated killing himself? Did he have it in him to murder his own wife and child?

Before the earthquakes, the fires, floods and storms, David Brewer had been a homicide detective. What he'd witnessed in those ten years had made the Apocalypse look like a sideshow. Still, the end of the world was only young. Things would inevitably get worse before they got better.

Is that the reason the dark thoughts have come? He knew what sort of future lurked around the corner. No, he wasn't a killer, he was a protector. Even if he wanted to throw in the towel, crawl into a dark hole, and let the broken world swallow him up, his heart wouldn't let him. He was a good man—most likely the only good man left in this God-forsaken place. The problem was the bad men out there just waiting to exploit the Apocalypse, and he couldn't let his family meet such an end. A mercy killing might be the only way to save them.

Rustling leaves made David turn. Behind him, about fifty yards away, a young deer stepped through the trees. It stood frozen, its legs spread wide, ready to flee if David made a move. He stared across the divide into its black eyes. The deer's nostrils flared, breathing David in. Gingerly, he eased his hand back into his pocket and felt the grip of the revolver.

That deer would feed you and the family for a week. Shoot it.

David imagined himself pulling the revolver free of his coat. The movement, he knew, would spook the animal. It would make a run for it. Even if he managed to squeeze off a round, the risk of missing was simply too high.

Then you'll fucking starve to death.

David's fingers ached from squeezing the grip. The deer blinked. At that moment, David remembered the boy he'd shot and killed at the 7-Eleven in Queens. His 9mm sent the boy into a spin, the bullet passing through his chest and into the display of juice boxes adjacent to the counter. He could see the pool of juice beneath the boy's vacant face, threads of blood turning it from orange to red in seconds. David felt an itch at his throat, but he dared not move.

You didn't miss then, so what's the problem?

David pulled the gun from his coat. The deer flinched and kicked its back legs, sending a flurry of dirt into the air. David lined up his arm for the shot, but the deer had already broken into a sprint, moving between the rocks. He squeezed an eye closed and trailed the beast.

Shoot!

David's ears popped as the round went off, the sound bursting out and rolling back in again an instant later. A bird that had been foraging on the ground took to the air. The slug slammed into a rock just as the deer passed it. By the time the echo of the gunshot faded, the deer was long gone.

David had just five bullets left.

2

Marci couldn't stop shaking. The wasteland surrounded her, its wide vista of death and destruction seeping through her skin to invade her every thought.

She tried to focus on the spot on the horizon where she had last seen her husband; the gap between the rocks on the landscape was a hole in her mind where only the worst possibilities resided.

Where is he? Why is he taking so long?

She needed him back by her side. If anything happened to him, Marci didn't know what she would do. If only he would listen to her. They had to move on, keep looking for other people; staying still only made things worse for them—for her.

David's stubbornness was something that Marci still struggled with. When they'd first met, he would always take things in his stride. Even his job as a police officer was something that he seemed born to do, like it was second nature. That all changed in a heartbeat. David's gentle-hearted, level-headed ways had been shed like so much blood. Marci so wanted her old David back, the dependable, strong man she'd fallen in love with, because she worried how she could survive without him.

Marci watched Kaley pace in a wide circle, the clouds of dust puffing off her heels. The girl, arms crossed tight over her chest, was staring at the ground.

"Your father said he needs you to get some firewood," Marci said.

Kaley grunted in response and kicked a stone off into the dirt. The girl was stubborn too, which frightened Marci even more.

"Kaley, we need to work together to help your father."

Her daughter offered her a fleeting glance full of scorn.

"Please, Kaley…"

The girl turned her back on her mother. Marci ran a hand through her hair in frustration and felt a twinge of panic in her throat. The open spaces of the endless nothing made it hard to breathe.

"Kaley… Your dad needs us, okay?" Marci picked at the edge of a thumbnail. "And we need him. We need to stick together and find a way out of here—"

Now Kaley turned and threw her arms into the air. "Mom, look around—there's nowhere to go!"

Marci took a deep breath. "There have to be people out there somewhere. We just have to go look for them!"

Kaley's laugh was condescending. She presented her mother with her back once more. "I don't want to go anywhere but home—but home doesn't exist anymore, does it?"

Marci wiped tears from her cheeks. "You're my home, Kaley— you and your dad. I only want us to be safe, and I don't feel safe out here."

"Well, Dad doesn't want to go anywhere, but feel free to leave if you want."

She felt her daughter's words like a knife to the chest. "Kaley…"

"Stop it, Mom, just stop it! I can't take it anymore! You and Dad are driving me crazy!"

Marci saw Kaley stand rigid on the spot, but still she kept her back to her. Marci's little girl was growing up, becoming an adult with her own emotions and voice, but this was not the way Marci wanted her to become a woman.

"I'm sorry, Kaley. I never wanted this to happen either. I'm only trying to give us a chance to survive."

Kaley turned to face her, and still the girl wore that same look of contempt. "Well, no offense, Mom, but let's leave the survival plan to Dad, okay?"

When Kaley's words stabbed her a second time, Marci's heart would have faltered, if not for the sound of a gunshot tolling through the wasteland.

When he returned to the campsite, David found Marci and Kaley cowering behind a tree. He saw the fear in their eyes. It was not unlike the look the deer had given him. Even after they recognized him and emerged from their hiding place, they remained uncertain.

"What happened?" Marci said, her fingernails digging into

her daughter's filthy sweater. "It sounded like you fired your gun."

Kaley pulled herself free of Marci's grip and glared at her.

"I saw a deer and tried to shoot it. I missed," said David.

Kaley sighed. "You missed?"

"I couldn't risk taking another shot. We might need the bullets."

His daughter threw out her hands. "So, what are we going to do for food now?"

"We'll find something—"

"What, berries again? Fuck that!"

"Kaley!" Marci said. "Don't swear!"

Kaley turned her back to them and kicked the dirt. "Jesus, Dad. You were a cop and you can't even shoot a deer."

David looked at the charred wood of last night's fire. "Where's the kindling?" He turned to Marci. "Didn't I ask you to tell Kaley to gather some firewood?"

Marci blanched. "I'm sorry. I heard the gunshot and panicked. Getting firewood wasn't a priority at the time."

"Well, it will be tonight when there's no fire to keep us warm."

Kaley stamped her feet. "Fine. I'll get it!"

Before David could speak, she stormed off in the direction her father had just come from.

"Don't go too far," he called after her as she stomped away from their campsite, fists clenched. Before her were great columns of jagged rock birthed during the end of the world. David turned from them and faced his wife. "Jesus, Marci, we have to stay focused. We have to stick to the plan: gathering food, maintaining the shelter, and staying put."

Marci wrung her hands. "I know! I know! I said I was sorry." She stepped toward him, hands reaching out to him for solace. "But maybe it's time to move on, try and seek out others—"

"No," David said. "We stay here, until the army or the government comes. We've talked about this, Marci."

Her fingers reached for his coat. "What if we can't find any more food? What if no one comes? We're in the middle of nowhere. How is anyone ever going to find us?"

David grabbed her by the shoulders and shook her. "What

if we walk to the nearest highway and there's a gang of thugs there, hmm? What if they kill me and then rape you and Kaley? Did you ever think about that?"

Marci cringed under his words, tears leaving lines on her dirt-encrusted face. It just infuriated him even more.

"You want me to protect you, Marci, then shut your mouth and do what I say, all right? The world doesn't exist anymore. It's just us"—he pointed into the woods—"and them."

Kaley kicked at the rocks and debris beneath her feet, sending plumes of dust into the air. Her anger swelled so fiercely she broke several branches off trees to fling them into the woods. She wanted to scream, but she purposely sat down in the dirt, chest heaving in deep breaths to try and calm down. When she wiped the tears from her eyes, the tips of her fingers twinged with pain. She turned her hands palms up and saw they were bloody and speckled with splinters.

"Fuck!"

She plucked the splinters out as best she could and wiped her palms on her pants. Sweaty, she plucked the beanie from her head and let her unwashed tangles tumble down, only for them to stick to her face.

All Kaley wanted was the world to go back to the way it had been before the earthquakes and the fires and storms. She missed her friends, and her dog Misty that they'd had to leave behind, most probably for dead. She missed coffee and her iPhone and reality TV. It had all been wiped off the face of the earth.

She recalled the day when the world turned upside down: the buildings falling to dust, gas lines rupturing in great balls of flame, people dying. Her dad had barely managed to get them all out alive, but now, here, stuck in the wasteland with no hope, she wished her father hadn't been so lucky.

The image of her father broiled inside her. Clambering to her feet and scanning the ground, she spied a rock as big as her fist. She hurled it as hard as she could, a satisfying grunt escaping her lungs. It soared and slammed into a larger mound of rubble, releasing a great cloud of dust. The slow descent of dust and rock from the mound calmed her, yet in the back of her mind, Kaley believed the red of the dust symbolized what the world was now all about —blood and death.

The adrenalin fading from her, she was suddenly overwhelmed by the desire to pee. She looked across the shattered terrain for a private spot.

"There's no one around for miles, your dumbass," she said. "Just pee already."

She undid the cord of her pants and squatted to relieve herself. Despite being alone, she still felt that niggling sensation that someone might be watching, that instinctive fear. Her father had taught her about stranger danger from a very young age. He had always been over-protective, using his job as a cop to patronize her. Despite all his warnings—and her instincts—Kaley knew she could never be in such danger out here.

Behind her a branch snapped. She turned in the direction of the noise, her eyes locked on the never-ending panorama of upturned earth. Her heart thrummed in her ears. Quickly, she pulled up her pants, gathered the broken branches she'd taken her frustration out on, and ran back the way she'd come, telling herself she had too vivid an imagination.

"**W**hat took you so long? I was worried sick," Marci said.

Kaley threw the branches and twigs on the ground next to the blackened remnants of the previous night's fire. David could see she was still pissed.

"I was fine," she told her mother.

"Well, just don't take so long next time."

"Will you stop treating me like a baby? I can look after myself!"

Marci stepped up to her daughter. "You are a child, Kaley. You're my only child!" Kaley softened, and David shook his head as his wife whined on. "I don't want to lose you." Marci's hands reached out, but the girl recoiled.

"Don't touch me!"

Marci looked as if she'd been slapped. "Kaley, please…"

David had had enough. He stepped between them. "Cut the shit, okay? This has to stop. Both of you." Still, he looked to his wife. "We don't have time to be squabbling amongst ourselves. We're just eking by here on scraps and you two want to snap at each other?"

Marci began to cry, and David cringed as that mask of desperation resurfaced. His wife dropped to her knees and plunged her face into her hands.

"I can't take this! I don't want to be out here anymore!"

"Marci—"

"No! No, you have to get us out of here! To a refuge or another town! I can't just sit here and wait in the hope that someone will find us!"

David held his breath and waited for Marci to stop crying, but his silence only made her worse. She gazed up at him, mucous running from her nose.

"David, please. You have to get us out of here!"

He could take no more of her begging. "Why do I have to be the one to do it, Marci? Because I'm the man, because I'm a cop? There's nothing I can do, do you hear me? I can't make everything right again! The world is fucked. We just have to learn how to live with it."

"Dad."

Kaley's voice pulled at him, but he ignored her to continue his tirade. He reached down and pulled his wife to her feet.

"Get up and stop sniveling, for God's sake!"

"Dad!"

He felt Kaley's hand pulling on his sleeve. He whirled on her, intending to give her a piece of his mind too, when he saw she was staring behind him, eyes brimming with terror. A new voice came from the trees.

"Well, isn't this just one big happy family?"

The expression on his daughter's face triggered David's old instincts. His hand slid into his coat pocket for the gun on meeting the newcomers.

Three men, all armed. The one in front was about David's height, six foot three, but stockier, and at least ten years older. He wore a singlet and jeans, despite the cold, and a well-worn baseball cap. A shotgun was slung over one shoulder, and a wry smile lingered on his lips. His companions were dressed more suited to the conditions, but they too wore caps and wanton looks in their eyes. One pointed a .44 Magnum directly at David, while the other nervously gripped the handle of a machete.

"How you all doing today?" the man in the singlet said. David saw him glance at his coat. "You might want to hand over whatever it is you've got in your pocket, boy."

David slowly withdrew his hand from his coat and held it up, palm out. "I haven't got anything. I was just trying to keep my hand warm."

"He's lying, Dale," the man with the Magnum said. There was ice in the man's eyes. David took a deep breath and exhaled. He was thankful his wife and daughter had been shocked into silence; the last thing he needed was for one of them to become hysterical and draw attention.

"Okay, okay—you've got me. I've got a .38 in there," David said.

The man David now knew as Dale smiled, revealing candle wax teeth. "Take it from him, Terry."

Terry, the man with the machete, stepped up and shoved his hand inside David's coat pocket. David took another deep breath; Terry smelled of whisky and cigarettes. He looked lighter in build than the other two, but his eyes blazed with enmity. The machete spoke volumes of Terry's violent tendencies. Terry extracted the revolver and handed it to Dale.

"Cute," Dale said as he examined the .38. He frowned. "You've only used one bullet?"

"Trying to conserve ammo," David said. He had to engage them and keep their eyes and thoughts on him.

"What'd you shoot at?"

"A deer."

"A deer? You nab him?"

"Too many rocks."

"Yeah, I see how that could happen. You're not going to hit much with this little thing." Dale opened the chamber, emptied all the rounds onto the ground, then threw the revolver away.

"What you need is something like this." He took the shotgun from his shoulder and snapped the barrel open. David heard his wife gasp. "This here would do the job. The buckshot covers a larger area. It won't kill a deer straight up, but it will wound him good. Slow him down."

"I know how shotguns work," David said, and immediately regretted it. Dale angled his head to one side, sizing him up. David glanced at the other two men and noticed that Terry was now eyeing his daughter.

"Oh, you do, huh?" Dale stepped closer to David, pointing the barrel of the shotgun at his gut. "So, what sort of damage would a shotgun do at this range, you think?"

Sweat trickled down David's back. He'd pissed Dale off now, not that it mattered. They were all as good as dead.

Bet you wished you'd eaten that bullet now!

Dale prodded David's belly with the end of the barrel. "What if I splashed your guts all over these pretty ladies here, huh?"

David swallowed. "Look, we don't have anything you need here. We barely have enough food —"

The barrel came up under his chin. Dale pushed the cold steel into his jaw. "We've got plenty of food, don't we, boys?" The pair nodded. "What we don't have" —his eyes shifted to Marci and Kaley—"is them."

Terry licked his lips. Marci started to cry.

"Marci, don't!" David snapped. Dale turned to look at her.

"Yeah. Don't cry, Marci. All we want is a little bit of company."

The man with the Magnum laughed and sidled up to Kaley. David saw his daughter cringe and squeeze her eyes closed as he snaked around her.

"Don't!" David said.

Dale pushed the barrel harder, stretching the skin under David's chin. "What'd you say, tough guy?" Dale's breath was like curdled milk. "You might want to keep your mouth shut or I might just blow it off your face."

Terry had moved around behind Marci. She stepped away from him, whimpering and keening, pushing out with her arms in a useless attempt to keep the man at a distance.

"Stay away from me!" she said, her voice rising to a shriek.

Dale flashed those jaundiced teeth and sidled up to her.

"You and I are just going to stand here and wait while the boys get acquainted with your women," said Dale.

The man with the Magnum tucked the gun in the back of his belt, grabbed Kaley's wrists, and flung her to the ground. David tried to move, but Dale pushed the barrel harder, forcing his head back.

"Uh–uh–uh!" Dale said.

Marci made a run for it, with Terry giving chase. Her screams mingled with Kaley's, as she struggled in the dirt against Magnum man's attempts to rip open her shirt. The sight made Dale chuckle.

"She looks like a fine piece of ass, Benji," Dale said to Magnum man. "You save some for me, now."

They're gonna rape your women, David.

David bent backwards off the end of the shotgun and, in one swift movement, slid to the side and reached out to lock his hands on the stock of the gun. Dale, caught off guard, tried to pull back on the gun, but David's grip was firm. As they pulled back and forth, the screams of David's women intensified.

"You're gonna die, boy!" Dale said.

Dale wrapped a leg behind David's knee and twisted, knocking him off balance. David fell, bringing his attacker with him. They hit the ground hard and rolled in the dirt, their faces inches from the wrong end of the shotgun.

"I'm gonna fucking kill you!" Dale said, spraying David's face with spittle.

David winced as Dale's knee jabbed him in the groin. Pain stabbed in his gut, giving Dale the opportunity to pin him to the ground with an arm to the throat. Through black stars of agony, David was now looking down the barrel of Dale's gun.

"Sayonara, motherfucker!"

David waited for the gun blast.

From nowhere a figure stepped behind Dale. Following a flash of steel, a red line appeared across Dale's throat. David had to close his eyes as a spurt of blood showered his face and chest.

As quickly as the figure had appeared, it moved on, retrieving Dale's shotgun. Wiping blood from around his nose and mouth, David saw the new stranger shoot Benji in the back, his coat suddenly resembling a cheese grater. Kaley, half-naked, and screaming, writhed as her would-be rapist slumped dead beside her.

Still the stranger was not done. With his tattered, hooded cloak fluttering behind him, he plucked Benji's gun from his corpse and ran to Marci's aid. Heart pounding, and the coppery tang of Dale on the back of his tongue, David sat frozen and watching.

In the distance, the stranger confronted Terry, who lashed out, swinging wildly with his machete. The stranger, light on his feet, avoided each blow with ease. The report from the .44 Magnum sounded like thunder, and Terry's head was a spray of red mist.

David remembered to breathe. He rolled onto his knees and sucked in air, listening to a calm and comforting male voice take away his family's screams.

Minutes passed before David heard the approach of the stranger's footfalls. He appeared in David's field of vision: cracked pale lips, the hint of an unshaven chin, shrouded within a dark hood. A crucifix dangled from his neck, almost hypnotically. The man spoke to him.

"Don't worry," he said. "The Lord sent me to find you."

Through the clicking of her chattering teeth, Kaley heard the voice of God.

"Stay very still, child," the voice said.

Kaley felt the man's hands on her face and she flinched. His fingers seemed to burn her skin.

"The sinners did not defile you, yet the Lord uprooted them like vile weeds."

The man stood, his silhouette a black obelisk that threatened to flood her mind.

"Who...who are you?" Kaley said, the question drawing blood from her split lips.

"I am His servant."

The stranger bent and lifted Kaley to her feet. She collapsed in his arms, a twinge in her knee almost buckling her. Blood oozed from a shallow cut across the front of the patella. The stranger placed her gently to the ground and crouched to examine the wound, pressing pale fingers along its edges. Kaley winced in pain.

"He shed His blood for us," he said. "It is fitting that we should do the same."

Kaley swayed, suddenly light-headed, but the stranger held her upright.

"Can you walk?"

Kaley nodded and tried to peer into the shadow of his hood. "Thank you…for saving us."

The stranger shook his head. "Only the Lord decides who shall be saved."

Kaley frowned, his words swimming inside her skull. She opened her mouth to seek more from him as her mother staggered toward them. One of her eyes was crimson with blood.

"You get away from her!" she told the stranger.

"Mom, no!" Kaley said, but her mother stepped between them.

"You be quiet," Marci said. "We have no idea who he is."

The stranger held out his white hands. "A mother's love is a gift from God."

"Why did you help us? What do you want?" Marci said.

The stranger bent his hooded head, his lips becoming a thin line.

"Answer me!" Marci cried.

Kaley gasped as a revolver appeared beside the stranger's head. She saw her father, grimacing in pain and rage, pointing it at the man who'd saved them.

"You heard her," David said. "What do you want?"

It all happened so fast. David was pointing the gun at the stranger's head and felt a searing pain in his wrist. The world turned upside down. When his mind finally caught up, he was on the ground, desperate for breath. David tried to get up but was pinned by the man's heavy boot on his chest.

As he struggled, Marci charged toward the stranger, screaming and holding a broken tree branch above her head. The stranger was already two steps ahead; he turned and caught the branch as Marci brought it down in a fierce arc. He plucked it from her limp hands and tossed it away. Kaley made her own move, but came to a grinding halt when the stranger unsheathed his knife.

"Violence begets violence," he said.

David studied him from the ground; he couldn't help but feel afraid of someone who was so clearly deranged. How can you reason with a man who seems to speak only in scripture?

"Okay, okay. Everyone just calm down. There's not going to be any more violence." He directed the last statement to his wife and daughter.

The stranger pointed the tip of his blade at David. After a moment he removed his foot from David's chest and took a step back. He sheathed the knife and put his hands to his side. David took this as a sign to very slowly get to his feet.

"Let's just all take it easy, okay?" David said again.

"All we want to know is who you are. Why won't you just tell us?" Kaley interjected.

"Kaley just leave it!" David said.

"No, Dad. This guy just saved us from being killed, but I still don't feel safe!"

David couldn't argue with that. He glanced at the stranger, who remained silent and unmoved. It was almost as if he was waiting for permission. David took a tentative step toward their savior.

"What are you doing?" Marci said.

"What's your name, soldier?" David asked the stranger.

The hooded man stood straighter. "Amos."

David's women exchanged worried glances.

"Why did you save us, Amos?" Kaley asked.

He turned to address her. "God has chosen you. He needs you to follow me."

"Excuse me?" Marci said, her voice shrill.

"The path to salvation is this way," Amos said, pointing to the east.

David ran a hand through his hair. The man's words frustrated him, but he had to stay calm. "Look, Amos, can you just stop with all this religious talk and tell us what it is that you want? We're grateful for you saving us from those assholes, but we're not about to simply follow you wherever it is you're going."

Their savior nodded. "There is a place, about ten miles from here. It is my sanctuary. I'd like you to come with me."

David immediately thought of his wife. He looked to her and saw the sheer relief in her eyes.

"You have a shelter? A house with food and water?" she said.

He nodded again. David hated not being able to see his face. Who would have so much to hide when there was nothing to hide from?

"What's in it for you, Amos?" David said. Amos' eyes were deep pools of shadow beneath the hood.

"I am fulfilling God's will, gathering up the hopeful." He glanced at the corpses of the men, their blood caking in the dirt.

David studied Amos' flimsy garb, a tattered collection of rags, tied and twisted together to create some sort of tunic or robe. "Well, I'd say you were a priest, but what sort of priest would kill?"

"David, please. He's only trying to help us," Marci said.

"I'm sorry, Marci, but I'm starting to agree with Kaley. It's hard for me to trust someone who won't even show their face."

Amos reached up and pulled down his hood. The scattered mid-morning light cast a dull hue across his milky features. His eyes shifted from side to side, but still remained locked on them.

Kaley gasped.

"You have albinism," David said.

Amos held out his hands. "I have been created in God's image, and a long time ago he gave unto me a message: 'Go out and find them and deliver them unto me.'" Amos quickly flicked the hood back over his face. "So, I have come to find you and take you into the light of His presence."

3

As he rolled up their worn blankets and gathered the dented cooking pots and utensils, David could feel Amos' eyes on his back, he glanced around furtively, trying not to be noticed. Although the hood hid his eyes, it was clear Amos was watching him, watching them all. Gut instinct told David to run, to get his family as far away from this man as possible, but rational thought stepped in. Or was it that little voice of angst?

Where would you go—another empty piece of wasteland? This guy saved you and now he's offering to take you to a refuge.

But David questioned whether Amos was telling the truth. He tried to see through the hood, to see his motives, to see if he was just as bad—or worse—than the other men. David turned and considered the corpses. Amos had made short work of them—and supposedly in God's name. A killer who kills for pleasure or need could be understood, but what of a madman? Amos claimed he was fulfilling God's will, that God spoke to him. David realized that the only difference between him and Amos was that Amos chose to obey the voices inside his head.

Kaley came to her side, and he noticed that she, too, was watching their savior intently.

"Did you ask him where he's taking us?" she said.

David's gaze went back to Amos. "He said it was ten miles east, which could be any number of places." He nodded towards the rocky landscape. "But there's only more of that in every direction."

"Do you think we should go with him?"

"Before, I would have said no, but if those guys managed to find us, then there's bound to be more like them out there. I don't like the vibe I'm getting from him, but maybe this Amos is our ticket to somewhere safe."

Kaley smirked. "I never thought I'd hear you say that." She frowned and stared at the bodies of Dale, Benji, and Terry. David reached up and held her hand.

"Hey, are you doing okay?"

Kaley blinked. "Yeah...I'm fine." She turned away quickly and went back to gathering the last of her things. David wanted to reach out to her, but Amos suddenly cast a shadow over him. The savior spoke from inside his cavernous hood.

"The road awaits."

Kaley kept her distance from Amos as they began the long walk into the wastelands. She walked alongside her father, but not as close as her mother, who seemed to carry a shadow of fear wherever she went. Amos walked before them with determined strides; his tall, hooded form negotiated a path that only he knew. From behind, Kaley could get a good look at the man who had killed her would-be rapists. He wore little more than rags. She could identify lumps of denim and cotton, all stitched together in a patchwork. His hood was more like a shawl, or a monk's robe, made from a thick fabric similar to burlap. Maybe her father was right: maybe Amos was some sort of priest. But then, like her father had also said, what priest would wield a knife?

She was glad the three men who tried to hurt her and her family were dead. They'd deserved to die. They would have raped her and her mother if Amos hadn't come along. She remembered her father: overpowered, helpless, and unable to help her.

Kaley wrapped her arms tight around herself, eager to hold on to her curiosity about Amos rather than the thoughts of the attack. *Thank God for Amos,* she thought. *Thank God.*

She drew away from her parents and approached her savior. Her father called out a warning, but she ignored him, instead sating her need to know more.

"So where did you come from?" Kaley asked Amos as she reached his side.

The hooded stranger turned his head briefly to acknowledge her. "South of here," he said.

She gave a nervous smirk. "Yeah, but where exactly?"

Amos ducked under a low branch, his face temporarily obscured, yet still looking straight ahead.

"North Carolina."

Kaley stepped around a rock in her path. "How…how was it there, when you left?"

"As bad as all the rest."

"Yeah, but were there lots of quakes there too?"

Amos ignored the question and simply continued along the path, his footfalls accentuating his silence. Kaley realized he didn't want

27

to talk, but then he rarely spoke unless it was to spout scripture.

"Did you have any family there?"

Her father interjected. "Kaley, for God's sake—"

"No," came Amos' response. His words were cold, but Kaley wasn't sure if it was loneliness she was sensing or something else. She decided to withdraw and move back to her parents. Her mother came to her and held her hand. Marci's eyes were sunken deep into her skull, the fear poisoning her features.

"What did he tell you?" she said.

"Nothing."

"I heard him talk to you."

"Yeah, I asked him where he was from and he said North Carolina, but when I asked him if he had any family back there, he said he didn't. That's all we talked about."

Marci frowned and stared at Amos' back. "So, he just wanders around helping people stay out of trouble?"

Kaley shrugged. "He goes on about God a lot. I think Dad might be right about him being a priest."

"Priests don't kill," her father said as he joined them.

She shrugged again. "Well, I don't know."

Ahead, Amos walked on, his shape occasionally bathed in fleeting sunlight.

"Maybe that's why he came out here to look for people?" Marci said. "He's looking for followers?"

David turned in front of them and they stopped. "Seriously, priests don't kill and they certainly don't carry knives. Look, we need to be extremely careful around this guy, until we learn more about him." He turned his eyes to Kaley. "And stop asking him so many damn questions. If we need to speak to him, I'll be doing the talking. Got it?"

"Yes, sir," she said, sighing.

Marci pointed ahead. "Look."

Kaley and her father turned and saw Amos had stopped and crouched low to the ground. He stared off into the distance. Kaley followed his eyeline and saw a deer nibbling at some leaves on a tree.

"Oh, you're shitting me," said her father.

Before any of them could react, Amos broke into a sprint in the direction of the deer. Kaley was astounded by his speed, how he leaped over shattered mounds of rock and exposed tree roots. The deer, alerted to Amos' sudden appearance, took off. Amos' pursuit never wavered as he kept pace with the animal, closing the gap effortlessly. Kaley saw a glint of steel as Amos unsheathed his knife, pulled it back over his shoulder, and threw it at the deer. The knife spun over and over, flashing gold in the sunlight, then stopped in the deer's neck, just beneath the jaw.

"That's impossible!" Kaley's father cried.

Kaley and her parents ran toward the scene as the deer staggered, blood spurting from the wound. Amos gained on the deer just as it fell. With a fluid, singular movement, Amos gripped the deer's muzzle in one hand, and gripped the knife with the other to slit open its slender neck.

Kaley, David, and Marci came to a halt, finding Amos up to his elbows in deer guts. Kaley thought its intestines looked like a bundle of purple serpents coiled on the ground. Their savior turned to them and with a bloody right hand, made a sign of the cross.

"Never fear, for God will always provide for you."

When Marci looked upon Amos, she saw the man who could take her family out of the darkness and into hope—if only her husband would see it too.

It was clear that she'd misjudged him, that her mind had been muddled with shock. Amos was a holy man, or a very devout Christian, a good Samaritan who was out to bring people to safety. He'd come out of nowhere and rescued them from certain death. She could hardly believe it. Now he offered to take them out of the horrible wastelands forever, yet David wouldn't have any of it, instantly erecting defensive walls and shutting out reason.

She studied Amos from afar as he stripped the deer carcass of meat. His ragged garb was just like her own—that of a survivor—but to her mind, a survivor who chose to protect himself with faith. The stranger was so quiet and reserved, something that

was at complete odds with the way he'd slaughtered the deer...
and those horrible men. Still, without those qualities, those skills,
they would all be dead. David could learn much from this Amos,
if only he allowed himself. Marci didn't find Amos' albinism to
be shocking; rather, she regarded it as another sign of his purity,
another sign that perhaps God was indeed watching over them.

The cold, grey sky turned blood velvet above the setting sun as
Amos butchered the deer.

He skinned the animal in venerable silence, the only sound
his knife scraping strands of meat from the deer's slender bones.
The butchery carried a hypnotic weight as Amos' hands moved
about the carcass with the deftness of an orchestra conductor.

Eventually David had to wrench himself away from the
spectacle to gather wood for a fire. He grabbed three thick
branches and staked two of them in the ground to make a crude
spit. He gave the third branch to Amos, who slid it through the
carcass, then placed it over the roaring fire. They all sat around
the blaze to enjoy its heat and inhale the smell of the sizzling
meat. Amos cut some into chunks and skewered them on sticks,
which he handed to his companions.

"Meat marshmallows," Kaley said.

"What?" Marci asked, smiling at her daughter's awkward
comment.

Kaley smiled. "Sorry, I was just thinking about the marshmallows we used to make when we went camping."

David smiled, too, recalling family camps from long ago. With
his job, vacations were all too rare, but it made those times when
they did go on vacation all the sweeter. He recalled his daughter
as a little girl with melted marshmallows stuck to her lips. He
looked at Kaley now and still saw that child in her. She was only
fifteen, but the end of the world had forced her out of naivety into
adulthood. He'd give anything for her to be a child again.

"Yeah, I guess they are like marshmallows," Marci agreed,
and she bit another chunk of venison off the skewer. "Mmm, but
this tastes a lot better than marshmallows." Marci gave a cautious
nod to Amos. "Thank you."

He nodded back and bit into his meal. David watched him eat and the word *diligent* came to mind. Everything Amos did was precise and reserved. His hunting display was impressive, and David had to bite back the urge to ask him where he'd acquired his knife skills.

"Yeah, thanks Amos," Kaley said.

Amos nodded in her direction and finished the meat on his skewer. "You must finish your meal and rest. Tomorrow we will undertake a long pilgrimage."

David wiped the grease on his trousers and chewed on his meat. "Good idea," he said. "I'll take the first watch."

"No," Amos said.

David frowned. "Okay, you want to keep watch first, that's fine, just wake me when you need to rest."

Amos shook his head, the hood wavering. "Unnecessary. I will watch over all of you."

David almost laughed. "Don't be ridiculous," he said. "We can take it in turns. You can't keep watch over us all night, you'll be exhausted—"

"God gives me the strength I need."

For a moment there was only the sound of the fire. David's patience with Amos' holy rhetoric was wearing thin. "Look, I appreciate you're a believer and all, and I appreciate everything you've done for us, but we have to work together here."

Amos flicked his skewer into the fire. "I know my cause."

The heat of the fire made David sweat. "For feck's sake, will you just stop it?" David heard the women interject. He felt the tension inside threatening to snap and he could no longer tolerate that blank, thin line of Amos' mouth. He got to his feet. "If you want to help us, that's great, but you're not helping yourself by ordering us around." The savior sat silently, which infuriated David more. "Why can't you just talk to us like normal human beings? You're wasting your time trying to convert us. I mean, it doesn't take a genius to realize there's no God here and, frankly, I don't think He ever was! We fucked this world up. This is just natural selection!" Marci urged David to sit, but all he could see was that mocking hood. "Take that off!" he said.

"Dad, stop!" Kaley said, standing.

"Lest ye be judged," Amos intoned.

David clenched his fists. "Marci, Kaley, pack everything up. We're leaving."

"No!" Marci said.

Amos didn't flinch as David turned on his women. "I told you to get our things! We're not staying with this freak any longer."

Kaley's face glistened with tears in the firelight. Marci's desperation returned, his wife pulling at her hair in a panic. Amos' voice wrenched them from their despair.

"He knows all, David," he said. "He knows all of his children; their fears and doubts, their sins—even yours."

David jabbed a finger at him. "You shut your mouth!"

"He can see into your heart of hearts, David. No one can hide from Him."

"Shut up!"

"Tell me about the boy you killed, David. Confess your sins, and He will forgive you."

David felt the cacophony of voices rise like a wave and he threw himself at Amos, grabbing at the savior's hood. He wanted to tear it apart, to tear the stranger's heart out. He pressed Amos to the ground with his left hand and rained down several blows with his right. Amos' hood fell back, revealing his alabaster face, expressionless, even as it was being beaten. He never said a word or cried out, just let David strike him again and again. David screamed in rage and hit harder, ready to kill him, when pain raced through his left arm. He tried to pull his arm free, but Amos held it tight at the wrist and twisted.

"Arrgh! Let me go, you fucker!"

David brought his right fist down. Amos caught it mid-flight. David felt his fingers compress inside Amos' grip and he buckled at the knees in agony. Still holding, Amos calmly got to his feet and gazed down with his soulless eyes.

"Penitence is beneath you, David. I had to be the one to bring you to your knees."

"Fuck…you…freak!" David spat at Amos. The spittle ran down his cheek.

The last thing David saw was Amos raising his right leg before the wall of unconsciousness: sharp and black and echoed by the cries of his women.

4

When Kaley saw her father's body slump to the ground and Amos turn in their direction, she screamed at her mother to run. Marci, stricken with terror, froze, eyes locked on her helpless husband.

"Mom! Run!" Kaley told her.

Marci's face contorted into a silent scream as Amos casually walked up and struck her with the back of his hand. She fell to the ground, and Kaley could only gape as Amos leant over her body to strike her again, knocking her out cold.

Kaley stood paralyzed by Amos' deception; he was a madman, worse than the three men he'd killed. Yet it wasn't until Amos turned those piss-hole eyes to her that she took her own advice and ran. Pulse pounding in her head, she sprinted through the wastelands, sucking in countless desperate panting breaths, and hearing the sound of Amos at her heels. Kaley pushed on, forcing herself not to think of him. She had to run, because if he caught her...

As she ran, the reasoning part of her mind begged for understanding. *Why would Amos kill those men, if he only meant to kill us? Because he's a psycho who thinks he's God?*

Kaley ducked and weaved between tree roots and rocks, but still heard Amos right behind her. She squealed as his fingers clawed at the back of her jacket. She was jerked backwards and reached out to grab at anything to keep her out of the madman's clutches. Her fingertips found a tree branch and she clenched it, but with a snap the branch broke away in her hands. She fell and instinctively turned on her knees, swinging the branch in a wide arc. Her arms shuddered when the branch struck the side of Amos' head. He cried out and stumbled, holding his skull. Kaley took the chance and raised the branch over her head. She wasn't sure she could do it, but then remembered her parents lying in the dirt and tensed her shoulders.

Amos raised an elbow just before the branch would have struck. He grunted in pain, but it was a sound defensive move.

With astonishing speed, he was on his feet and prying the weapon from Kaley's grasp. He tossed it away and wrapped his hands around her slender throat. She squirmed and shrieked at the sting of his fingernails in her skin.

"All children should come to the Son," Amos said.

"Let go of me..." Kaley said. She lashed out with her hands to punch and scratch at Amos' face and arms, but he held her and shook her fiercely. She could only watch, helpless, as Amos whipped his head back and slammed it into hers, plunging her into a sea of unconsciousness.

Kaley woke to a darker hell that had been waiting for her.

The skin of her wrists burning, she looked down to see her hands bound with rope. Her heart slammed against her chest. She tried to pry her hands apart, but the thick strands only cut in deeper. As she twisted in vain and stared into the dark, she realized the rope was connected to a much longer piece which snaked away from her. She followed it with her eyes to discover it was wrapped around her mother's waist. Alongside Marci sat her father, who was also tied up. He wore a defeated look, his face smeared with blood. He regarded Kaley with guilt-soaked eyes.

"Don't say or do anything," he told her. His voice was thin. Kaley nodded just as their captor came to address them.

"I will carry you into God's graces," Amos said. "He is waiting for you, and if you repent, He will take you into His arms."

Kaley's father spat at Amos' feet. "You're gonna have to drag me, asshole, because I'm not going anywhere with you."

Amos ignored David and looked to Kaley from his shroud of shadow.

"We're all sinners in His eyes, Kaley, you should know this. Original sin, from when man abandoned Him in the Garden of Eden." He gestured to the stark grey wasteland around them. "He has abandoned His flock, save for a few. If you follow me, you will find forgiveness."

David scurried across the ground toward her, the rocks and soil grinding beneath his knees like bones in an ossuary. "Don't listen to his bullshit, Kaley!"

Amos' hand lashed out, a glint of steel swiping the air. David screamed and toppled over. His hands clutched his face and after he pulled them away, they were slick with blood. A long red slash ran across David's cheek like a mock smile.

"You fuck!" David said, spitting blood as it ran into his mouth. "I'll kill you! I'll fucking kill you!"

Amos sheathed his knife and picked up the length of rope that connected them. The savior pulled hard, and they all lurched forward, Marci coming awake with a cry. They had no choice but to be led through the desert once more. Thunder rumbled off to the west, gusts of wind scattering dust to the air and into Kaley's eyes. Lightning cracked the sky like a malfunctioning strobe light. It made walking difficult, escape impossible. They couldn't run anywhere in the dark.

Kaley listened to her father wincing in pain, spitting and cursing. Her mother's sobbing started all over again. They were puppets in Amos' hands, mannequins being dragged through an asylum of dust and darkness. Kaley tried to quell these somber thoughts, but anxiety coiled tightly inside her. Her mother's voice wrenched her away, and Kaley turned to see Marci trip and fall in the velvet dark. Amos hauled Marci up, steadied her, and brushed away her tears with a pale finger.

"Christ fell three times on the way to the place of skulls." Despite Amos' rough-handedness, Kaley was sickened that he would take a moment to touch her mother's cheek so gently. "Take strength from that," he added.

"Fuck you and your Jesus shit!" David said.

Amos drew his knife again, walked behind David, and slashed him across the back.

Her father doubled over in agony.

"Stop it!" Kaley said. "Leave him alone!"

Amos simply sheathed his blade and looked down upon her father. "The Lord sent his only Son to shed His blood for our sins, David. You will do the same."

Until the dawn came, Kaley and her parents trudged the long path to redemption.

There was much shedding of blood throughout the night.

5

Marci walked through the dark, shedding tears in time with the constant outpouring of her husband's blood.

She wanted to hold him, but she was within the prophet's cold shadow. Marci could only sob as hope dwindled with each step of Amos' self-imposed march across the wastelands.

She'd been a fool to believe their *savior's* intentions were ever pure. She should have listened to David, to Kaley, and not to the sliver of false hope that now stabbed accusingly at her soul.

Marci watched her husband stagger through the dirt like a reanimated corpse. The trail of blood drops he left behind were rubies in the moonlight. She clutched the rope that connected her to him.

"David…" she said, keeping her voice low.

David wavered on his feet to the left, tried to straighten, only for his back wound to buckle him all over again.

"David…"

"Mom. Shut up."

Marci turned to her daughter and saw that mask of judgement in the moonlight.

"He's bleeding to death!" Marci said.

"Shut up or he'll hear."

Marci looked up at the prophet as he led them ever forward. She took the chance to creep closer to David and recoiled at the sight of the glistening, spreading patch of wet darkness on the back of his coat.

"David?" she whispered over his shoulder.

Her husband stumbled, his feet barely lifting off the ground. She heard his rasping breaths.

"David. I'm sorry I ever doubted you."

She reached out, touched his shoulder, and instantly recoiled at the sticky touch and the sight of her palm shining dark red.

"Mom, get back!" Kaley hissed.

Marci stared at David's blood. She'd seen it before. He'd lost so much then and survived. Perhaps he would a second time.

"I love you," she told him, and then fell back into line, taking her place in Amos' exodus of pain.

With each step, David felt Amos' knife slash his back all over again. Each grimace of pain reopened the laceration on his face, shedding fresh blood, a vicious cycle from which only death could release him. It would likely be his own death before Amos'—unless he summoned the strength to escape the bonds. But Amos was smart and had taken down the strongest link in the chain. He had won them over with his rescue routine, but in the end, he was simply removing the competition.

David's right shoe caught on a rusted girder, concealed beneath the dust like a snake. His stagger sent a jolt of pain up his back. He stood straight as a soldier, clenching his teeth against the searing of his skin. Rivulets of fresh blood soaked into his stiffened shirt, plucking at him like a harpist's deft fingers. He heard the concern in his daughter's voice.

"Dad, are you okay?" she said.

He strained his neck to look at her over his shoulder. "Don't worry…about me. Just do as he says…and leave the rest to me."

Kaley nodded, but the look of defeat on her face belied any confidence in his assurances. He turned away from her and scanned for Amos, who strode about ten feet ahead, his hand tight on the rope. David looked down at the coils around his wrists, the fibers blazing red, the skin beneath cracked and raw. He twisted his wrists again and winced, but pushed down the barbs of pain which followed to study the trail his blood had created. If Amos wanted him to bleed, he was willing to oblige if it gave him any chance of escape.

The wasteland was sparse where they walked, the few rocks and collapsed building frames like sentinels against the dull grey light of morning. David wondered how far they were from a road; going by the remoteness of the area, he realized he would have to get free of his bonds sooner rather than later. As to what he would do after, he wasn't sure.

How do you take down a crazy motherfucker with a knife who can drop you on your ass in a heartbeat?

You get to the knife first.

It wasn't a good plan, but it was a plan nonetheless.

David bided his time and continued to twist his wrists inside the rope, dreaming of the new blood to come.

David shuffled through the dust, step by step, towards confrontation. Amos seemed to walk blindly, determined to stay in a straight line, stepping over obstacles rather than around them. The madman was focused, obsessed. David planned to use that to his advantage to get within striking distance. He just hoped his wounded body wouldn't fail him. As the minutes passed, David closed the gap; he could almost taste the vengeance in the back of his throat.

Amos stopped. David halted too, with Kaley and Marci following suit. Amos stood on the spot with his back to them. It wasn't until the stranger turned his hooded head ever so slightly to the sky that David discovered he was listening for something. This was the moment. David had to take it. He clenched his hands into fists and stepped towards him—

The world shuddered beneath David's feet. Marci screamed and the echo of her terror mingled with the roar of the earth. David lost his balance as the ground shook and shifted. A great cracking sound almost burst his eardrums as he dropped flat on his stomach.

"Earthquake!" Kaley cried.

All three of them came together and huddled on the shivering ground. Around them, great towers of rock thrust out of the ground by previous tremors began to teeter. The vibrations in the earth generated a miasma of red dust. Withered tree roots buckled and split, the bones of the earth fracturing into splinters.

David looked ahead and saw Amos still standing amongst the carnage between two crumbling rock spires. The rumbling from the quake grew louder, so loud that David could no longer hear his family screaming. Following another crack an enormous black fracture tore the surface apart, not far from where Amos stood. The crack resembled a long black vein but only for a moment, as it quickly widened to a chasm. David hoped Amos would fall into it, but to his astonishment, the madman seemed unperturbed and, worse still, impervious to the carnage being wrought.

Unable to sustain its own weight, one of the rock columns toppled. There was a great wave of air beneath it as it fell. The ensuing dust cloud overwhelmed their vision. Yet, if Amos was to perish, David was determined to watch it happen. Squinting through the dust, he caught sight of Amos' shape, still standing in the same spot, his arms raised to the sky.

The rumbling began to subside, but not before something emerged from within the chasm. The dust cloud seemed to thin out and slide towards the rising shape. There was another rush of air, but this time in the opposite direction. David watched the dust swirl upwards, turning and coiling into an incredible funnel—a tornado!

The tornado formed out of the chasm's depths right before Amos. It pulled in dust and rock, it pulled at Amos' tattered robes, but still he seemed made of lead. The whirlwind untethered itself from the earth and soared away from them to the north, taking tons of the barren earth with it. Amos and his captives were left miraculously unscathed.

With the dust settling, and the tornado just a smear on the horizon, Amos came to them. David could sense the spite emanating from within his hollow hood.

"Do you still think that this is not the Lord's work?" he asked David. "Or can you finally see that God only spares those who truly believe."

The highway was a black gouge in the fractured earth, an ancient scab. Kaley watched the road fade into the ashen horizon and felt lost; where once the sight of a road would have given hope, she held only despair. The road wasn't bare, there were a dozen vehicles, abandoned like beetle carapaces. Some had been crushed by rockfalls, others burned black by more human forces. Trails of smoke rose to join the thick grey canopy overhead. Shafts of sunlight blinked on and off in the distance, nothing more than promises. Kaley had hoped to see a town on the other side of the highway, but there was only another dying woodland. Amos stood at the roadside and stared into these woods, waiting with practiced patience.

Kaley was about to call out to him, to seek an explanation for what had happened during the earthquake, when her mother unexpectedly pulled down her trousers and squatted to urinate into the dirt. As Marci did her business she sobbed, but much more silently than expected, as if to herself. She was losing her mind to fear. Still Kaley couldn't pity her mother or even her father when she looked at him, hunched over, his coat blackened with dry blood. It was hard to feel anything at all. He stank of blood and piss. She wanted him to fight, but despair and failure seemed to have claimed him, too.

Kaley clenched her fists and called out to their captor, her voice carrying across the void. "What are we waiting for?"

Amos turned to face her and slowly twirled the rope around his arm, like a first mate reeling in an anchor. Kaley and her parents were drawn toward him and she worried that soon his knowing mouth and secretive shadowed face would devour them all.

"My flock," Amos said.

"What the fuck are you talking about?" her father said. Slights seemed to be all the fight he could muster.

The branches rustled, but not from any wind. From the shadows between the drooping trees, people emerged. Men and women of varying ages, dressed in similar drab clothing to Amos. Six in all, they walked to him, smiling widely and embracing the prophet, one after the other. The hugs were brief and reverent. Once the greeting was over and done, Kaley felt the newcomers' eyes converge upon her and her family.

"Who are these three?" one of the older women asked Amos, her eyes narrowed.

Amos considered his captives. "More of the Lord's lost children."

One of the men looked at the ropes around Kaley's wrists. "You tied them up?"

Amos pointed to Kaley's father. "This one is truly lost. He is blind to his sins. Sadly, he has corrupted his wife and child."

Amos' flock blessed themselves. "May the Lord save them," they said as one.

David spat on the ground. "Look, I don't know who you all are, or who you think Amos is supposed to be, but he's been holding us prisoner. Does that seem very Godly to you?"

Amos smiled thinly from beneath his shroud and then turned to address his followers. "God's good work," he said.

"God's good work," they replied as one.

David laughed. "Jesus Christ—he's brainwashed you, too!"

Again, the newcomers made the sign of the cross. "Forgive him who has blasphemed!" one of them said. The rest repeated the exultation.

"Now you see what I have been up against," Amos said. "But fear not, my brothers and sisters, for we shall take these three and their souls into our church and we will do what we can to save them."

"Yes, Amos," they said.

As Kaley was pulled into the woods with Amos and his people, any shred of hope she had dwindled and died.

6

They arrived at the "church" following a ten-mile hike through the woods. The structure, what remained of a four-story warehouse or office building, consisted of crumbling concrete and shattered windows. The church had been shaken by the earthquake and now leaned to the left. To David, it was a skeleton of what society once used to be, converted to a madhouse for a group of religious freaks at the ass end of history.

He and his family, their hands still tied, were urged through the severed chain link fence that surrounded it. He saw some of Amos' people lingering, felt their contemptuous eyes. There were elderly couples, young families with small children, all of them wearing the same meagre grey tunics or shawls, undoubtedly selected by their leader. Paradoxically, they looked well-nourished and rested. He guessed they could relax when God took care of everything. When they stared at him, David stared right back. Little did they know that he would be free and ready to make them all pay for his family's imprisonment.

He was halted at the main entrance by Amos. David looked over his shoulder to study the interior of the building. Plastic tarps fluttered in the breeze, tables and chairs were stacked high in corners, and children played in puddles of filthy water that dripped from cracked pipes in the ceiling. The wastelands suddenly looked significantly more inviting than Amos' temple.

"This is what a five-star hotel looks like these days, I guess," David said to Amos.

"God told Peter that on him He would build His church. The people are His church."

David shook his head. "When are you going to stop with this bull? These people need food and shelter, not a fucking Sunday school."

Amos pulled back his hood and his pale, scarred face glistened in the grey light. "Repentance is what they need, just like you. Once they repent, God shall set them free."

David studied Amos' scars, his bloodshot eyes. "So, what— you all missed out on the tickets to the Rapture, is that it? Doesn't that mean you're a sinner too?"

Amos smirked. "We're all sinners in God's eyes, David, some more than others. Now, come inside and pray for your soul and the souls of your family."

The chapel was on the top floor. Amos untied him from his wife and daughter and walked him up the internal staircase where children played with crudely carved wooden dolls. Their parents congregated on each floor, whispering, praying— blinding themselves to the truth. The chapel was vast, with half a dozen rows of chairs and on the wall, a large cross crafted from ash tree bark. Even if he did believe, David wouldn't feel like sitting in this cold, dead room to worship. Amos stood in front of the cross, blessed himself and knelt before it. A snigger escaped David's lips. Amos stood to face David, his eyes red with resentment.

"You like to mock God, David?"

"God is a delusion," he said. "Do you honestly believe that if God existed, he would have destroyed his greatest creation?"

Amos sat in one of the chairs. "God has destroyed the earth before and, just as He did then, He is testing us anew, testing our faith. We turned our backs on him so this"—he gestured outside to the slowly dying world—"is our test, our punishment for forsaking Him."

"God is not going to save you or anyone. You can only save yourself."

Amos stood, walked to David, and began to untie his bonds. David took a deep breath.

"He tests the non-believers as well," Amos said as he unthreaded the knot. David couldn't believe his luck, that Amos would be so foolish. Still the prophet went on. "He tested you back then in that convenience store too, when you killed that boy."

David felt his fingernails dig into his palms. "You shut up! You shut up about that! I don't know how you know, but don't you say another fucking word!"

The rope slid to the floor. The two men's eyes were locked.

"I know about Marcel because God told me about him. He told me about you in a dream, David, in a vision. God told me to find you because He was going to test you."

David punched Amos in the jaw. The savior toppled backwards into the front row of chairs. David took the opportunity and jumped on top of him, raining down blows to his head. He had to knock Amos out, had to get the upper hand before he could react. David watched the blood run from the prophet's nose into his mouth and the sight of it only encouraged him to hit his captor harder. Amos looked up at David and smiled, all bloody gums. David raised his right fist but before he could bring it down, Amos reached up and gripped his coat. The prophet pulled himself up and slammed his pale head into David's face. David heard a sickening snap, and a burning pain blazed across his nose. He recoiled and gripped the bridge of his nose. His fingers slickened with blood.

"You broke my fucking nose!"

David fell to the floor as Amos kicked him in the ribs. He rolled in a bid to stay out of the prophet's reach, but Amos closed the gap and kicked him in the side once more, knocking the air from his lungs. When David rolled onto his back, Amos' heavy boots struck his chest and head. Blood filled his mouth, and he feared he would choke. His body was wracked with pain; the gash on his back reopened, his ribs wrenched with every plea for breath. Kicks from Amos' boots left him paralyzed. He curled up in the fetal position to try and protect himself, but this only urged the prophet on. The beating stopped, but only momentarily as Amos reached down to grip David's trouser leg and pull him along the floor and out of the room. The cold of the concrete seeped through his clothing and seized the skin of his bloodied back. He tried to writhe free of Amos' hand, only to be stilled by the sound of the prophet's voice in his ear.

"God welcomes the penitent into His house. You may enter when you are ready to seek his forgiveness." David was lifted to his feet, but fell limp in the savior's arms. "You will be tested. You will become like Daniel in the lion's den. You will cry out for God's forgiveness, and He will redeem you."

David spat blood in Amos' face, the color stark against his alabaster skin. "Fuck you."

Amos backhanded David across the jaw so hard he fell backwards. For a moment he floated on that cushion of air until he met the hard concrete stairs. David tumbled back over himself. His strained ribs snapped, as did his left knee. David's screams echoed inside the narrow stairwell, but Amos was far from done. Three more floors waited below, and David would have to reach the depths of Hell before he would be allowed to rise again.

Kaley's heart thrummed out a constant beat of fear.

She'd watched Amos drag her father away, leaving her and Marci still bound and with his clan. Their eyes craved her, as if they bored through her skin to feast upon her soul. She was surrounded by people who seemed anything but human.

Kaley and her mother were taken to the second floor, where the followers seemed to have congregated en masse. Filthy mattresses and sheets lay scattered about the floor. It proved cleaner than Kaley had first imagined, yet from outside came the stink of rotten food and human waste, which pushed any physical sense of cleanliness from her mind. Amos' people were living in squalor, sustained only by his words, the words of a maniac pretending to be God. Her father's logic was now impossible to deny.

Her mother came to her side, trembling and grabbing at her. "Where did he take your father?"

"I don't know."

"What are we going to do?"

Kaley stepped away, but Marci followed, their roles now reversed. Kaley was unsure her mother would survive this new madness, and if her father succumbed to Amos' will—or his blade—then Kaley didn't believe she would, either. She walked a few paces to a far wall and focused on its blank canvas rather than the leering eyes of Amos' kind. Her momentary silence was shattered from a hand on her shoulder. She whirled about, ready to scold her mother when she saw one of the group standing behind her—a young woman, about her age. The girl held out a piece of grey cloth.

"You need to put this on," the girl said.

Kaley stared at the relatively clean piece of fabric. "What?"

The girl averted her gaze. "You're part of the family now. You need to wear this."

Kaley knocked the tunic out of the girl's hand. The follower gasped and recoiled.

"You get the fuck away from me!"

The girl scrambled to pick up the piece of clothing from the floor. Her eyes, wide with shame, looked to the others. Kaley wondered why she would be afraid of them if they were all family.

"I'm not wearing anything of yours," Kaley told them all as they watched with furtive anxiety. "I'm not one of you people. You got that?" You can all go to Hell!"

The young girl retreated with the fabric clasped tight to her chest, but not until she offered Kaley one final rebuff. "You need to wear the clothes, or Amos will not be pleased."

"Fuck Amos!"

The family flinched at Kaley's words, with some of the adults even reaching out to cover their children's ears.

Someone cried out from the floor above, followed by a rumbling on the stairs. Screams of pain rolled around the stairwell and into the room, down and down until Kaley could no longer deny the identity of the voice. She pushed away from the wall and ran to the entrance to the stairwell. She gasped at the sight of her father lying on the floor, his body bloody and broken. Amos stood over him, the prophet's knuckles flecked with the same blood.

"Dad!" Kaley tried to go to David's aid, but she was held back by a sudden throng of Amos' followers, who converged upon her with greedy hands. Kaley screamed as they pulled her back. Her father was dragged away down the stairs, his back and head slamming against each grubby step.

"I'll kill you!" Kaley shrieked. She kicked and howled against the group, which ripped the coat from her back, their fingers tearing at the fabric of her sweater and shirt beneath. Kaley watched through tear-streaked eyes as the followers turned their attention to her mother. Marci cowered while she was stripped, her shaking hands trying to retain some semblance of dignity. Two women had the foul grey tunics, the uniform of the family, and pulled them over the heads of mother and daughter. Kaley thrashed, kicking out and spraying the followers with her spittle. She managed to knock one old woman to the floor and would have kicked them all but stars suddenly burst behind her eyes when a man slapped her hard across the face.

She was part of Amos' family now, whether she liked it or not.

7

David stepped through the sliding doors of the 7-Eleven convenience store with his gun drawn. The boy pointed something at the cashier, demanding money. David tried to focus, to keep himself under control, but the edges of his vision were blurred by the bottle of self-imposed ignorance he'd swallowed. He'd been drowning his sorrows when the 10.30 call came through and he was the closest responding officer. But on entering the store and expecting to find an armed teenage boy threatening staff and customers for cash, he beheld the prophet Amos instead.

The back of Amos' hand brought David back to cold reality: a dark, dank basement, swarming with cockroaches, dripping with filthy water. David thought he had died, and the room was his tomb. Amos' shadowed visage sliding into view above told him otherwise.

"The Lord God is the one true judge, David," Amos told him. "Only He can hear your sins and grant forgiveness." Amos' hand wrapped around David's jaw and squeezed. A tooth shifted inside, sending shivers of pain through him. "So, speak, child of God. Tell Him your sins."

David opened his mouth to speak, but blood slurred his words. He spat a glob onto the prophet's shoe.

"You know God sent His only Son to bleed for the world," Amos continued. "In doing so, the sins of man were forgiven. Yet for two thousand years hence, man chose to forget that sacrifice and, for two thousand years, man kept on sinning and sinning. It was when man abandoned God's existence completely that He abandoned us and sent His plagues of judgement. Do you honestly believe that all this destruction—the firestorms, the earthquakes, the floods—are just acts of nature, the impacts of global warming? God is angry and just like before, when He ordered Noah to build the ark, He has tasked me to rid the world of the last of the sinners."

David shook his head and laughed. His ribcage seized from the exertion, but it was worth it.

"I've said it before and I'll say it again: you're fucking insane." He laughed anew, and his throat gargled with blood. He gladly spat again.

Amos crouched beside him. "In the days before the end, God granted me visions, so many visions. I could suddenly see into the hearts and minds of the sinners who'd survived. He showed me their secrets and lies and ordered me to track them down. Do you know how I knew these visions were truth?"

"No, but I sense you're going to tell me."

The prophet pulled down his hood. His white face shone with tears. "Because the first sins he showed me…were mine." He reached out his hand toward David. "Do you want to see my sins?"

Amos' fingertips touched David's forehead, and the world swirled backwards in time. The Earth was whole again, swarming with six billion plus people. Nestled in one city was a church, a vast building of sandstone and secrets. Its exterior façade shielded the ugliness within, but Amos' touch now allowed David into its very dark heart.

David saw a boy draped in a white robe, a red sash tight around his waist. His face was as stark as the robe. He stood in the sacristy shaking and crying. Around him on the walls, the faces of Christ and the Virgin silently watched the proceedings unfold. The boy had trusted this Man of God, had heeded his every word. That trust had been torn asunder when the priest removed the boy's robes and forced himself upon him.

Each time the priest disrobed, the boy wondered how God's own Son and Mother could watch such horror, yet never intervene. The boy had declared his faith in God by serving his priest at the altar—Was this the reward for such obedience?

Years drifted by in heartbeats. The boy grew, came to believe that God was punishing him for committing carnal sin, for compounding upon the sin he was born with, when Adam and Eve fled the Garden. It wasn't that God didn't want to intervene. He simply couldn't, because Man had brought it upon himself.

The priest stopped raping the boy when he turned fifteen; it ended as it had begun, in the confessional, with the priest forcing him to promise that his sins were sacred, forever sealed by the sacrament of reconciliation. The boy carried that secret like a stone. It pulled him down into a black ocean of despair. He retreated from life: from his family, friends, and even love. He chose to reject love and embrace death.

On his 21st birthday, the boy stood on a chair in his unkempt bedroom, placed his head through a noose, and stepped off into his personal Armageddon.

In the darkness between life and death, the boy saw the Earth crack apart like a wound with cities falling into lacerations of molten lava. He saw continents become dust and millions dying in pain and terror. Tidal waves washed their corpses into the sea, tornadoes scattered others into the air like leaves, falling and falling to paint the soil red. In that instant the boy witnessed God's wrath.

The boy woke in the rubble of his apartment, the vision becoming prophecy. The beam he'd tied the rope around had shattered when the earth split, granting him a stay of execution. When he eventually climbed out of the dust and looked out the window to behold the remnants of the world, he realized that God had always been watching. The boy understood he was to be God's last prophet on Earth.

From that final day until now, the visions came as often as the tsunamis that lashed the coastlines of every nation. He sensed God's plan in the smell of the blood of sinners and heard it in their screams. The sights and sounds called to him by name, and that name was Amos.

David came to in the dark. His body ached with each breath; there was only pain and the memory of the images Amos had shown him. He rolled on to his side, to find the prophet sitting in the corner of the room, the hood around his face full of darkness.

"What did you see, David?" said the hollow hood.

David dragged himself to a sitting position and hissed at the pain that came with the movement. He slid along the floor on his backside until he reached the comfort of the wall. The inside of his skull pounded with infected blood.

"Nothing," he said, wiping bloody drool on his sleeve.

"You cannot lie to me," Amos said, shaking his head.

"I'm not lying."

Amos climbed to his feet, and David tried to straighten in readiness for an attack. He licked his dry lips with a parched tongue. "You can try to beat it into me all you like, but I'm not going to change my mind."

Amos titled his head, considering David. "This is God's test—a test of your faith."

"You know I don't believe in God."

"Oh, but you should if you want to survive, lest sin claim you."

Jesus, aren't you tired of this shit?

David winced as the voice interrupted his thoughts; it had been some time since he'd heard it.

"Perhaps it's not about testing your belief in Him," Amos said. "Perhaps it's about testing the faith of others."

David thought of Kaley and Marci. "You stay away from my family."

Amos bent down and tucked a strong hand beneath David's armpit to lift him to his feet. David cried out as fresh agony burst in his ribs and back. His vision doubled, and he slumped into the prophet's shoulder.

This fucker is going to kill you and your family—take action!

"Come," Amos said. "Let's go and test the faith of the people."

The dry cloth of the tunic pricked at Kaley's skin. She wanted to tear it off, to stand naked rather than wear their garments, but they watched her too closely now. After they'd been stripped and forced to don the uniform of Amos, Kaley and her mother were marched back to the worship room. They were sat on opposite sides of the room. Kaley surmised that this had been done in order to prevent any further misdemeanors.

"You become accustomed to the feel of it after a while," Kaley's chaperone said.

Kaley instinctively shuffled away from the girl. "Don't talk to me."

The girl offered her hand. "I'm Angela."

Kaley looked at Angela's hand as if it were a piece of rotting meat. "I don't care who you are. I don't want to talk to you."

"It just takes time," Angela said, smiling thinly and shuffling closer. "The clothing, the praying, the confessions. It's better than being out there." Angela looked to one of the broken windows. Kaley followed suit, could just make out the tips of the trees. Beyond that were the vast empty wastelands of collapsed civilization.

"I'd rather be out there than in here with you people."

Angela's mouth parted in mute shock; the look of horror on her small face caused Kaley's skin to crawl.

"What?" Kaley said.

"You were almost raped, weren't you?"

"Excuse me?"

Angela swallowed. "When Amos found you, you were about to be raped by those men."

Kaley saw the image of Benji looming atop her, his tongue like a worm sliding across his lips.

"Yeah... So what?" Kaley said. She crossed her arms.

"So, Amos saved you from certain death. That's what Amos does, that's why he's here: to help us find God."

"You really believe he's real, don't you?"

Angela nodded. "You've seen the storms. You can't deny that He is with us, and that we need Him to survive. Amos says God has given us a second chance, that if we reveal our sins and beg His forgiveness, then He will grant us a new life on Earth."

Kaley pointed at the window. "Earth is a shit-heap. There's only dust!"

Angela smiled and looked around the room at her kindred. "Not here. Here there's plenty of food, water and clothing—and love."

"Love? You've got to be kidding, right?" Kaley stared at every-one praying or watching their conversation. "All I see is fucking crazy!" She felt Angela's hand on her shoulder.

"I was like you before. It was just me and my two brothers, Jacob and Riley. Our parents had been killed in a rock fall during a tremor after the first quakes hit. We wandered around for weeks scrabbling for food. One day, we awoke to Amos in our camp. That's what he does. He goes out and finds survivors and then brings them back here to start a new life."

Kaley glanced around the room. "So where are your brothers, then?"

"They're dead."

Kaley's eyes widened. "What? What happened?"

Angela lowered her gaze. "The same thing that will happen to your father—unless he repents."

The worship room smelled of sweat and iron, a metallic tang that sat deep in Marci's throat.

How Amos' people could tolerate such a stench she didn't know, but it was obvious that fear kept them in check—the same deep-seated fear that had taken hold of Marci the moment Amos had asked her husband about the boy.

Marci couldn't comprehend how the prophet had known David's secret. Amos' knowledge, his very words, seemed to carry some sort of power. She thought back to the earthquake, how Amos had stood in the center of the destruction with no fear in his heart. Could he really have been sent by God? Marci had thought about God since she was a child and remembered the stories from Sunday school: stories of an old all-knowing, all-seeing God who destroyed His enemies with floods, fire and plagues. Could this destruction truly be God's doing?

She looked across the room to her daughter who was talking to one of the cultists, a young girl about Kaley's age. The girl was chatty, enthusiastic, and all smiles. Kaley was the complete opposite: frowning, morose, and impatient. Marci considered the other cultists around her and they too looked content and obliging. She started to wonder if Amos was right and that David might have been wrong.

No. Amos was cruel and violent. He'd hurt David and killed those men, those sinners. Amos had punished those men for the sins they were about to commit. What, then, of David? Would Amos punish him, too? What sort of punishment does someone who has lived their life hiding their sins receive?

Marci flinched as a man and a woman approached her and sat down. The pair offered her thin smiles and penetrating stares.

"Hello," the woman said. "You must be Marci."

Marci pulled her legs in and sat up straight against the wall. A crawling wave of fresh panic erupted across her skin.

"My name is Jim, and this is my wife, Vera," the man said.

The husband and wife appeared to be normal. They were about forty years of age. Jim's hair was turning grey at the temples, and crow's feet had taken up residence near Vera's eyes.

"What do you want?" Marci said.

Vera reached for Marci's hand, but she pulled it away. "Oh, Marci, there's no need to be frightened. We only want to help you and your family."

Jim turned and nodded in Kaley's direction on the other side of the room. "I see your daughter is making friends with Angela."

Marci saw only worry in her daughter's eyes. "She's your daughter?" Marci asked them.

"Oh, we're not Angela's real parents," Vera said. "The Lord took them when He began the Reaping, but she's like a daughter to us, isn't she, Jim?"

Jim nodded. "We're one big happy family here. Amos has given us so much: a place to live and worship, with food and water."

"Hope is what he's given us," Vera added. "And all we had to do was admit our faults as human beings."

"That's all?" Marci said.

Jim and Vera nodded together.

"That's all," Vera said. "God is forgiving; he wants all of us to join Him in Paradise."

Jim placed a hand on his wife's shoulder. "As long as we come to Him with open hearts, seeking forgiveness."

Marci thought of David with Amos. The prophet wanted David to admit his sins, but David had committed no sin in the eyes of the law. He was simply doing his job as a sworn officer.

"But my husband hasn't committed any sins, none of us have," Marci said.

Jim and Vera smiled again.

"Marci, we're all sinners," Vera intoned. "We were born with original sin passed down from Adam and Eve. The only way to receive forgiveness from original sin is through death."

David took the stairs one searing step at a time. His left leg, leaden and twinging with shards of pain, barely managed to clear the top of each step. The sound of his scraping boots echoed inside the stairwell, as if to mock him.

He sensed Amos at his back, ever urging him forward with his presence alone. David wished the prophet would end his suffering, but that was hardly in Amos' nature. No, Amos wasn't ready to finish with him just yet. Despite his agony, David still reeled from the visions Amos had shown him, but he couldn't acknowledge them. He didn't know how he'd seen Amos' past. The most logical conclusion was that Amos had drugged him with a hallucinogen and suggestion. Still, the last thing David wanted to do was fuel the fire of hysteria, lest it infect him too.

What the visions had revealed was the cause of Amos' fixation of faith. A boy, molested by a priest, who was reborn at the end of the world to believe he had the voice of God inside his head.

When are you going to grow a pair and kill this fucker?

The voice had returned, little David prodding at him like an angry insect out for blood. The pain seemed to have amplified it. David could never take Amos out in his current weakened state. He was bloody and broken, his spirit spent. Yet his conscience would not relent.

Stop being a fucking pussy and do it! Turn around, take hold of his head, and snap his fucking neck!

David stopped at a turn in the staircase, his head swimming. Amos gave him a nudge.

"I need a minute," David said.

"You can only make time for God—"

"Fuck, can you just give me a minute?"

The prophet fell silent and stood waiting. David was surprised; he thought for sure Amos would correct him.

"Are you listening to the voice in your head, David?" Amos asked.

David's jaw slackened. "How do you—"

The prophet's lips were hypnotic. "When we connected, I heard that voice, just as you witnessed the visions I showed you."

David shook his head. "No…"

Amos walked past. David could only stare at that cavernous hood in disbelief.

"How long have you been hearing that voice?"

David squeezed his eyes closed now, refusing to look at him. He gripped the railing and tried to pull himself up the stairs. Amos blocked his path.

"Did it start when the end came…or before?"

"There is no fucking voice, and I didn't see any visions. You're insane and nothing you say or do is going to change that! So, let's just get this execution over and done with."

8

As the sun set, Amos' followers decorated the chapel with candles and knelt, hands clasped, before a table upon which sat a wooden box. Kaley and her mother were forced to kneel amongst them, paying reverence to some relic they couldn't see or comprehend.

Kaley couldn't help but feel drawn to the dull incarnadine glow of the candles and kerosene lamps tinged by the setting sun on the walls. She felt trapped in an amber daydream. Kaley scanned the faces of Amos' people, saw their eyes locked on the stained timber box. She wondered if the relic inside would be a crucifix or some last copy of the Bible. Then she realized they wouldn't keep such a precious object hidden away inside a box; it would be on the wall or in Amos' possession. She looked from it back to the followers and saw her mother kneeling with them. She, too, stared at the box. Marci was so weak that Kaley feared she had surrendered her will to the church already. She called out to her mother in a whisper.

"Mom?"

Marci's eyes never wavered. Kaley leant out from the line carefully to call her again when Amos entered the room, dragging her father behind him. All eyes turned to the savior. Kaley gasped at the state of her father. She wanted to cry out to him, but the furious expression on Amos' face urged her to stay silent and still. She could only watch as the prophet pushed her father to the floor, beside the table where the sacred box sat. Cracked moans of pain emanated from her father's lips. *He's finished*, she thought.

"Welcome, Children of God," Amos said, pulling back his hood and standing behind the box. "It's been some time since we have gathered as one."

The followers nodded. It was like a pantomime of a church ministry in the Deep South. Amos continued.

"It has been many a day since we have confessed our sins in the sight of the Lord." The prophet placed his hands on the box. "We need to remind ourselves more often of the fate which God has bestowed upon us, the divine fate, the chance to begin anew and wipe away that which befouls our souls as the Lord Jesus Christ did when He gave His life for us on the cross."

The followers exhaled a collective *amen*. Kaley stared at the box and then at her father. He smiled gently and gave her a wink. Did he have a plan?

"It has been longer still since the Lord remade His world in this new image. The ground has gone silent, and I feel that this is a sign that it is time for us to go out and begin his new Eden."

Amos gripped the sides of the box, and Kaley saw his knuckles turn white. He was angry.

"Before we begin, we should remember those who came before, the ones who followed in Jesus' footsteps and bled for their sins." Another resounding *amen*. Amos turned and pointed to David. "God, in his wisdom, has brought us newcomers, new sinners who we can cleanse." The prophet looked at Marci and then into her own eyes. "I will ask for you to pray for them now, to give them strength. I want you all to guide them with your every action and show them what they must do in order to truly seek forgiveness."

The followers climbed to their feet, and Kaley felt a hand on her elbow encouraging her to stand with them. She turned to find Angela at her side again.

"It's time," the girl whispered.

"Time for what?"

"For confession."

Two followers stepped forward from the line, a man and woman. They stared deadpan at their leader and spoke in almost robotic tones.

"We wish to offer the sins of Maximilian," the man said, and the line all turned to look at an elderly man standing, face downcast, amongst the line.

"What are they doing?" Kaley said, with worry rising in her voice. "Are they volunteering people?"

Angela put a finger to her lips. Kaley turned aghast back to the gathering.

"Max told us he'd fondled a little girl when he was seventeen," the woman said.

Maximilian stepped out and spoke into his chest. "It's a grave sin."

Amos nodded and his followers concurred. The couple, and Max himself, took a step back into line.

"Oh my God," said Kaley. She felt sick and clamped a hand over her mouth. Still others wanted their turn to confess the sins of their peers in front of the prophet. A young man put an arm around the woman standing beside him.

"Jennifer had sex with another man," he said. "She told me it happened the night before the Reaping."

Jennifer nodded in acknowledgment. "I know adultery is one of the Commandments. I beg God's forgiveness so that Alex might live."

The crowd spoke as one chorus of supplication, calling out to Amos for the Lord to forgive them their transgressions. Kaley couldn't believe the madness she was witnessing.

As Amos calmed the followers, Kaley looked to her father. Still he just sat on the floor, a shattered man. Surely, he hadn't given in now. Her eyes were drawn then to Amos, who opened the lid of the box and reached inside.

"A year ago, God sent me a sign. He showed me His plan. I was a sinner then, without faith or hope, so I did not at first believe what I saw. It wasn't until He led me to my first sinner that I discovered the path He had laid out for me."

Amos lifted up his hands. Kaley watched the object emerge as if in slow motion: a withered tuft of gray hair, blotched, peeling skin, the vacant upturned eyes, slackened lips nestled in a tangled grey beard, then finally, the blackened, gaping throat. He held the severed head high. Kaley screamed.

"This is the face of the first sinner, the so-called man of the cloth who defiled me. Yet, this is also the symbol of my pledge to the Lord—the relic of my reconciliation and in turn, God's pledge to me of my forgiveness."

Kaley tried to pull away, but Angela and two others held her fast as Amos held the head out towards his people.

"Now what pledge will you make in order to be forgiven?"

The followers turned to face each other and from cloth satchels they retrieved lumps of rock, wooden stakes, and shards of glass half-wrapped in grey tape. Kaley felt her heart pounding in her throat, instinct shrieking at her to flee, but then her father's voice overtook her every thought.

"Oh, fuck, what did you do?" Kaley turned at the sound of the voice and saw her father crawl out to stare at the severed head. "You killed the priest? Oh, Jesus! God!"

Kaley was shocked that her father seemed to know who the dead man was. She watched as David hobbled closer to Amos and then lashed out to grab the head from the prophet's grasp. The head slipped from Amos' fingers, hit the floor with a thud, and rolled towards the congregation.

Screaming with rage, David launched himself at Amos and knocked him to the ground. As her father wrapped his hands around the madman's throat, the followers began to murder each other in the name of Lord.

Amos' children writhed on the ground, stabbing, bludgeoning, strangling. They were in a frenzy, mobbing individual members and shedding their blood across the chapel floor. With each killing blow, the murderous followers chanted the same phrase over and over.

"Lord, accept this sinner's sacrifice! Accept their blood so that we can have a place in your new Eden!"

The sinners' blood spattered over their grey tunics and pale, expressionless faces. Kaley cowered in the corner, screaming, but none of the victims made a sound; they gave their lives willingly, in the belief that God would spare the rest.

Kaley saw her mother rocking on the floor, arms wrapped tight around her shaking form. She wanted to go to her mother, but the killing spree kept her on the other side of the blood-soaked room.

"Mom!" she cried. "Just stay there!"

A couple fell on the floor in front of Marci. The man, who Kaley recognized as Alex, had his Jennifer pinned down and was stabbing her in the chest and throat with a screwdriver. Blood jetted upwards and saturated Marci's legs, but she didn't even flinch.

"Lord accept this sinner's sacrifice," Alex proclaimed.

On the other side of the room, another man slit a young girl's throat. Maximilian was struck over the head with rocks by a trinity of followers. He fell backwards and shattered a window. Some of the attackers picked up the shards and plunged them into his torso until he was dead. None of his killers seemed concerned about the cuts to their own hands.

"Accept this sacrifice so that we can have a place in your new Eden!"

Through the tumult Kaley feared they would soon turn their attention to her and her mother. Weren't they sinners in the eyes of the followers, survivors who needed redemption? A young girl was struck in the face with a piece of steel pipe before Kaley's eyes. The girl fell to the floor at Kaley's feet. Kaley shrieked when she recognized the girl as Angela. A man straddled the limp body and slammed the pipe into her skull over and over until it came open with an audible crack, spilling the girl's brains onto the floor.

Fear snapped inside Kaley, and she made for a run across the room. She shoved past a group of bloody-faced followers, heading for the stairwell, only to trip and fall flat on her face. Feeling something pulling at her leg, she turned and saw Amos grasping onto her feet, dragging her toward him.

"No—get off me!" she said. She kicked at his face, but he only sneered. A moment later his visage became contorted with pain. Her father was pounding his fists into the prophet's back.

"I told you not to touch my family!" David said.

Amos released Kaley. She scrambled free and pressed her back against a wall. She watched her father slam his fists into Amos' back and ribs, and she willed him to win. Her hopes were dashed when the prophet bucked David off and flipped him over. Before David could react, the prophet was wrapping his alabaster hands around his throat.

"Are you listening to that voice now, David?" Amos said. "Do you hear it? It's telling you what you must hear. He's been calling to you all these years, since you killed that boy! Now you have to listen to Him. This is what is meant to be, David—you and I, the conduits of Good and Evil. The final battle to decide the fate of the world."

Her father's face turned blue, and she saw spittle forming at the corners of his mouth.

"Dad!" cried Kaley.

David let go of Amos' hands and reached up to claw at the prophet's face. Amos squeezed tighter. Around them, the followers continued their madness, slaughtering the sinners until dozens of dead lined the floor. In their butchery, one of them knocked over a stack of candles and lamps. Liquid fire sprayed across two corpses. Their ragged tunics burst into flame. The fingers of fire spread to quickly engulf the next body and the next, sweeping across the floor like a snake to snatch up the wooden chairs. Soon the room was ablaze, and the survivors of the interrupted carnage dropped their weapons and ran for the stairs. Kaley made a move to help her father but he turned and locked her with his gaze. Blood oozed from a gash above his eye.

"It's okay," he told her. "I'll be okay."

Kaley hesitated, her chest tight with fear.

"Run…" he said. "Go…!"

Then he turned back to Amos, reaching up one last time to push his thumbs into Amos' eyes. Blood spurted from the sockets, and he howled in agony. The savior and prophet let go and stood, clutching his face. Blinded, he staggered straight into the flames, which greedily latched onto his robe. He became a tongue of flame and overwhelmed, he fell to the floor, baptizing David with the same fire.

Knowing her father was dead, Kaley ran for the stairs—and her life.

Smoke coiled into the night sky as the Church of the Apocalypse burned. Kaley sat on the ground and watched the tongues of flame dance from the windows, living and then dying into the black, taking the souls of the sinners and the enlightened with them.

She thought of her father burning within the chapel and wondered whether his soul would rise to Heaven, whether God would accept him. What sort of God would have permitted all this death? The greasy smell of burning flesh permeated the air, filling her lungs. She coughed, and the action seemed to temporarily disconnect her from the shock wracking her body. Wisps of ash swirled around her, and she trailed them with her eyes. The landscape answered her question. Holding on to hope only led to madness; Amos was proof of that. There was no hope because God had taken it all away. In truth, Kaley now believed no one here was meant to live and, for a moment, she considered walking in to the inferno to join her family. Kaley closed her eyes and tasted the salt of tears. In her mind she saw the face of her father smiling back. Kaley loved him and she wished she'd told him that before he gave his life for her and Marci.

The thought of her mother drew her gaze back to the inferno. "Oh, no—Mom!"

The sound of footfalls behind her made Kaley jump and she turned, expecting to be set upon by the surviving followers. She gasped when she saw Marci standing before her.

Kaley had never been so happy to see her mother and she clambered to her feet and held her for a long time. The woman trembled in her daughter's arms.

"It's okay, Mom," Kaley said. "It's over. Dad stopped him."

Marci slackened in Kaley's embrace. "Your father..." she began. "I think he was meant to die here."

Kaley let Marci go and took a step back, frowning in confusion. "What?"

Marci wiped her eyes. "I don't know what he...Amos...said to your father, but he seemed to know about the shooting."

"What shooting? Mom, what are you talking about?"

Her mother's lips quivered. "It happened years ago...when you were little. Your dad was called out to an armed robbery. He got into a shoot-out with a boy, a fifteen-year-old boy. Your father's bullet killed him and the boy's..."

Kaley's eyes widened. "Dad was shot?"

Marci nodded. "It hit him in the neck...grazed him. The doctors said if it had been a half inch to the left, he would have been killed. We never told you because we didn't want you to worry."

Kaley looked to the building once more and saw the embers of her father and all the other victims fading away. A deep ache settled in her heart.

She surveyed God's new Eden, one that seemed destined to go on without humanity. So many lives lost, and it didn't matter whether they had faith or not. Kaley turned to her mother and contemplated the end acutely for the very first time. Before, the only hope she and her mother had had was David, but Kaley hadn't realized it until he was gone. Looking out upon the ruptured, dying earth, she knew for certain that neither of them would survive without him.

Kaley reached out and held her mother's hand and together they walked out into the wilderness to embrace their fate.

"Don't worry... the Lord sent me to find you."

BLACK DAYS AND BLOODY NIGHTS

The moon's shadow was enfolding the sun when the first call reached Dr. Sam Carlton's phone.

He sat alone in his car, parked on an overpass overlooking the Atlantic, mesmerized by day turning to night before his eyes. It wasn't that he couldn't hear the phone ringing, he simply didn't want to take the call.

When the sound became too much for the confines of his car—and his skull—he answered it. His wife Kate's frantic breathing echoed in his ear.

"It's a tumor," she said. "In her front...frontal lobe. In our little Sara's head."

Sam opened the driver's side window and peered up at the celestial majesty unfolding. Below, about one hundred people had gathered on the beach to observe the lightshow. The shadow of the moon crept steadily across the face of the sun and Sam couldn't help but imagine a cancer cell casting a shadow across healthy cells in his daughter's brain.

"How much time does she have?" he asked Kate.

Her breaths became heaving sobs. "Six...six months. Oh, God, Sam... Isn't there anything we can do?"

The lunar shadow, now engorged against the light of the sun, stretched out over the ocean, the golden sands and the assembled crowds. A shadow on the world. A shadow on his little girl's brain.

"Sam? Are you listening to me?"

Sun and moon converged, light and dark colliding millions of miles apart in a dance with the void.

"There's nothing we can do," he told her.

He knew he should turn away to protect his sight, but the eclipse, now a ring of fire, had cast the world in a blood-red light.

"What?" Kate cried. "How can you say that? You're a doctor! You work for the fucking CDC for Christ's sake. You deal with disease and death every day. There must be something we can do for her!"

The eclipse sat unbroken in the sky. Transfixed. The moon should have passed by, returning the noonday sun to its former glory. Yet the world stayed drenched in blood.

"Kate, are you seeing this?"

"What? Seeing what?"

"The eclipse..." Beneath him the crowds on the beach began to cry out in panic. "The sky, Kate, look at the sky."

The engaged signal rang out. Kate was gone, stricken by a grief that was yet to come. Their daughter was going to die and yet the sky was falling. Why couldn't Kate understand the magnitude of what was unfolding—how insignificant their problems were? When his phone rang a second time, he quickly answered it.

"Kate?"

"Sam, it's Morgan. Something's going on at the Hilton. Reports of a contagion on the seventeenth floor."

Tears streamed down Sam's face as he watched the eclipse sit frozen, unwavering. People scattered like ants on the beach, desperate to flee something that was unavoidable.

"Morgan? Have you seen the sky?"

"For feck's sake, Sam. That's the least of our worries right now. We need you at the Hilton now. I can't send you a chopper. The whole damned sky has been declared a no-fly zone, but a convoy is on its way to your location. Just get here, Sam. Just get here."

The military convoy escorted Sam through the chaos of the freeways. Mass panic had taken hold, impending doom hovering undeniably above the populace. The Humvees weaved between the mangled wreck of an SUV, its occupants, a mother and father and their two young children, strewn across the asphalt. Sirens rang out in unison with the screams. All Sam could think was how pointless it all seemed—racing against time when all time and space seemed to have ground to a halt.

As they jostled through the carnage, Sam's phone rang, his daughter's name flashing on the screen. She would need him, he knew, but could he give her the hope she wanted? The soldier driving, seemingly annoyed, glanced at him in the rear-view mirror. Sam picked up the call.

"Daddy?" Sara was already crying.

"Honey, I can't talk long."

"Do you know what's happening? Why is the sky all on fire?"

"I don't know, honey. Is your mom there with you?"

Wet sobs came down the line. "Daddy, I don't want to die."

Sam swallowed hard, stared at the columns of smoke rising from the city center. He didn't know how to comfort her in a world that was crumbling.

"Everything will be okay. I'm sorry, honey, but Daddy has to go now."

When he ended the call, the soldier in the passenger seat turned to speak to him. "Coming up on the site in five clicks, Dr. Carlton. I've been instructed to tell you this situation is a Level 4."

Sam glanced between the gaps in the buildings as they sped along 34th Street. The eclipse was a watchful eye, black and calculating.

"A Level 4? Have none of you seen the sky?"

The Humvee came to a screeching stop at the Hilton, the lower half of which had been encased in a circus-tent-sized sarcophagus of steel and Perspex. Morgan met Sam outside the main entrance to the hazard area, sweating inside a cerulean blue HAZMAT suit.

"I need you in a suit and up to the seventeenth floor, stat, Sam," he said. "We've got to find out what's going on up there."

The eclipse's crimson glow seeped into the Hilton's façade. Sam turned to see the eye lurking over his shoulder.

"You want to find out what's going on in here?" He pointed

to the eclipse. "Does anyone know what the hell is going on up there?"

Morgan looked at the spectacle. "I'm told that NASA's best and brightest are onto it."

"What can they possibly do?"

Morgan gripped Sam's shoulder. "Sam, I need you to focus. The sky isn't our problem. What's happening on the seventeenth floor is." Sam stepped into the tented corridor as Morgan persisted. "Sam, are you okay? Can I count on you?"

A montage of Sam's daughter at her recent birthday—her tenth birthday—flashed against his mind's eye. Sara riding a pony in the front yard while her friends watched; Sara's nose bleeding; Sara flopping in the grass. The only difference was that the sun was the eclipse, staring hungrily.

"Yes," Sam said. "Do we know what we're dealing with?"

Morgan came to his side as Sam was helped into a HAZMAT suit. Sam had known Max for more than a decade and he'd never seen him perspire so much inside a suit.

"Apparently a man who looks like death."

The seventeenth floor had been cordoned off, sealed tight inside its Perspex carapace. In the center was Room 267, the alleged source of the contagion. The door to the hotel room had been removed and replaced with a thick sheaf of floor-to-ceiling opaque plastic which was zippered to the door frame. Through the plastic shield Sam saw the murky shape of a seated figure, bathed in the glow of the eclipse, head bowed as if in reverence. Sam and Morgan picked up their medical cases, carefully unzipped the plastic door and stepped inside.

Shadows filled the four corners of the room, the only illumination being the phenomena outside. The naked figure sat on a chair opposite the end of the bed, facing the only window, which looked out onto 34th Street. To the figure's right was the entrance to the bathroom. There was nothing else of note about the space, only the man in the chair. Sam followed Morgan, who approached the patient. Sam determined to give the situation all his attention and not be distracted by the burning sphere hovering above the city.

"Sir?" Morgan said, cautiously circling the man. "My name is Dr. Maxwell. I'm with the Center for Disease Control. We understand you are feeling unwell?"

Sam turned on the light switch. Morgan cried out as the overhead lights flickered on, revealing the man's true state.

The patient was trembling uncontrollably, his eyes wide and fixed on the eclipse outside, almost hypnotized by its splendor. In his hands he held a large, tattered book, its yellowed pages bearing a series of foreign symbols and imagery. Sam, keeping his distance, recognized none of them. The man's skin was grey and mottled with a patchwork of blackened veins, as if a colony of mold had taken up residence just below the surface.

"Jesus Christ. Sir, can you hear me?" Morgan reached out to touch the shoulder, but the patient screamed, startling the scientists.

"Help. Help. Help." The man sucked in deep mouthfuls of air.

"Sir, can you tell me your name?"

"Help. Me."

"Yes, we're here to help you. Can you tell me your name?"

Sam walked past them around the bed to an open dresser drawer containing the patient's belongings. He picked up a wallet and flipped through it.

"His name's Martin Howard-Phillips of Rhode Island. Age 43, occupation: archaeologist. There's a plane ticket here, too. New York to Tehran return, dated yesterday."

Morgan nodded and gently squeezed the man's shoulder again. "Martin? Martin, can you understand me?"

Martin Howard-Phillips shivered, teeth clattering together. "B-b-b..."

Morgan gripped his patient's wrist. "His pulse is racing and thready." Next, he retrieved a temperature gun and scanned the man's forehead. "Temperature of 102. It's like catatonia, or some form of paralysis, but then his skin bears the hallmarks of infection." Morgan glanced down at the scrawl in the book and reached to take it. "How about you give me that and we try and get you to stand up?"

Sam watched as Morgan tried to take the book out of the man's hands, his colleague pulling as the patient clenched it tight.

"Jesus, he's got a vice-like grip on this thing," Morgan said. "Martin, can you let go of the book…"

"Morgan, be careful, you don't want to tear your suit."

Martin's lips quivered. "B-b-b…" His eyes rolled back in his head. "B-b-book!"

Sam willed himself to go to Morgan, to try and get him to give up on the book. Every instinct in Sam's body told him that the patient's bizarre state and what was happening in the heavens were connected.

"Morgan, stop!"

"B-b-b-book!"

Sam's eyes met Martin's, the jaundiced sclera reflecting the eclipse beyond, creating a new, dark, yet incandescent, iris. A string of blackened drool slid from the man's lips, onto the pages of the book. The symbols began to bleed in the fluid.

"This isn't paralysis…" Sam muttered.

Morgan let out a sigh and ceased his tug-of-war. "What?"

"It's control."

Morgan backed up and tried to slow his breathing. Sam could tell he was frustrated; panicked, even.

"What do you mean, *control?*"

Sam pointed to the window. "For God's sake, Morgan, look at the sky? An unexplainable celestial event is happening right above this city, and we've got an unexplainable contagion going on here before our eyes."

Morgan blinked at the eclipse. "So, what… This is some kind of mania?"

"I'm not sure, but it can't be coincidence. I mean, look at that book. It looks like some sort of…spell."

Morgan chuckled. "You're not suggesting…?"

"Look at the sky, Morgan." He thought of the cancer growing inside his little girl's head. "It's like the fucking world's coming to an end."

Morgan considered the man, the eclipse, the book, and Sam watched the realization wash over his face.

"The book… You think it's causing it?"

Sam crouched to study the book. It was ancient, looked like it should fall to pieces in Martin's impossible grip but was defiant. The arcane symbols shone in the red light of the frozen sun.

"Maybe." He observed Martin's shaking, venous form. "What if he brought this book back from Tehran and it…affected him?"

"Like he dragged this out of some tomb and inhaled some ancient spores?"

"No, like he simply read from it—translated it—and caused the eclipse."

Morgan turned his back on him. "I…I don't know what to say to that. I guess the only person who can tell us what happened is Martin Howard-Phillips—"

Morgan's pondering was cut short by the patient's scream. The scientists backed away as Martin's jaw unhinged, releasing something akin to electronic feedback, high-pitched and deafening. It ended almost as quickly as it began, but the man's mouth remained open, like the entrance to a cave.

"What the fuck was that?"

Sam swallowed, his frantic breath fogging up the inside of his visor. "Martin?" he said, carefully approaching him. "Martin, what happened to you in Tehran?"

Martin's eyes rolled to consider Sam, like the bulbous eyes of a wooden clown. The flesh inside his mouth was patched with clusters of black veins.

"Do you know something about the eclipse? Is it the book? Was there something in the book that made it happen?"

Morgan crouched down, too. "Hey, remember when I almost lost it before? Well, now I'm telling you to stop."

Sam locked eyes with his patient, ignoring his colleague. "Martin? Martin, are you still in there? Can you tell me what happened in Tehran?" He looked down at the pages. "What do these symbols mean? What do they say?"

A hiss rose from deep within Martin's throat like wind in a tunnel. Syllables and clicks. An ululation from the other side.

"The gn'th'bthnk yogshugg riseth. The mgfm'latghnah ng n'ghft ephaidrench nilgh'ri orr'ee ph'nglui crimson gn'thh."

71

"What the fuck?" Morgan gasped.

Sam stood, his mind afire with the determination to run, but he pushed it down. "Who is speaking?"

The echo rolled up from Martin's hollow core. *"Gn'th'bthnk yogshugg."*

Morgan grabbed Sam's arm. "I don't know what the fuck is going on here, but I say that we sedate this freak, get him on a gurney and get him into a psych ward."

Sam turned on his associate with a cold stare. "He can't leave here, Morgan. We can't leave here. Not until we make it stop." He faced Martin once more. "Whoever is inside Martin, please, I want to understand you—I need to understand you, but your words are lost on me."

Morgan backed up against the wall, resigned to watch. "Are we scientists now, or are we exorcists?"

"Gn'th'bthnk yogshugg ephaiai language ot broken."

The thing inside Martin lifted his right hand, like a puppeteer, up to his open mouth. Before their eyes the unhinged jaw snapped shut, biting off the tip of his index finger. Morgan howled in horror as the digit spilled from the man's mouth to the floor. Sam recoiled as Martin used the bleeding end like a pen, scraping across the page. The crude words that issued forth read:

BLOOD

MOON

RETURN

Sam sat mesmerized as the puppet-man who was Martin Howard-Phillips, kept writing in his own brackish blood. Words becoming symbols—circles—repeated on the page and then the next page and the next. Through the sound of bone on paper, Sam heard his friend Morgan reciting the Lord's Prayer.

"It's the eclipse," Sam said. "I…I think I'm talking to whatever caused the eclipse."

The puppet-man's chest swelled with air and new words came in a language they could understand. One word after the other, stilted, yet deliberate.

"I. Have. Waited. Eons. Sleeping. In. Darkness. I. Was. The. First. Before. The. Light. The. Blood. Of. The. Cosmos. The. First. Cell.

The. First. Life. The. First. Death. All. Come. From. Me."

Morgan stepped warily to Sam's side. "You have to stop this!"

Sam shook his head. "No, I need to know how. Why." He addressed Martin's inhabitant. "Did you cause the eclipse?"

The entity's growl filled the room. "The. Day. Is. Mine. The. Night. Is. Mine. My. Chains. Broken."

Sam pointed to the book, splattered in Martin Howard-Phillips' blood. "This is a book of ritual, then? Martin found it in Tehran and somehow…activated it. The book is the key to your release? What's holding the sun and moon in the sky?"

"Conduit. All. Will. Worship. As. Before."

"Is that what you want—to rule us?"

Martin's open mouth receded into a smile. "N'ghftog yah'or'n-anah ng gn'th'bthnk n'ghftyar. Black. Day. Blood. Night."

The shrill of a ringing phone cut through the palpable terror in the room. Morgan, startled, quickly answered it, picking up his medical case to step away into the bathroom. Sam barely acknowledged Morgan's departure. His every sense was locked onto the thing inside Martin.

"Please, you have to make me understand," Sam said, staring into the thing's eyes. "Are you God? Is this the end?"

Martin the puppet-man turned his head, the first physical movement since they'd first entered the room. It spoke, more black blood, spilling out from between the man's cracked lips.

"I. Can. End. All. Suffering. All. Pain. Even. Sara."

Sam stood, his flesh prickling with cold beneath the HAZMAT suit. "What did you say?"

The thing followed him with its blank gaze. "Sara. Can. Live. The. First. Life. Forms. To. Emerge. From. Your. Sea. Were. Microbes. My. Cells. My. Blood."

"How do you know about that? How do you know about my daughter?"

Morgan re-entered the room, the phone still to his ear. "Sam! It's all over the news! NASA… they're saying that there's something on the surface of the moon…something hatching."

Sam looked to his colleague, noticed the syringe in his other hand. "What?"

Morgan rushed at Martin Howard-Phillips, grabbing at him. Sam, terrified of the possibility of what was in the syringe, how easily a needle-tip could puncture their suits, stepped between them.

"Morgan, don't! Stay back!"

Morgan halted, clutching the syringe like a knife. Condensation obscured most of his face, but there was no mistaking the fear and rage in the man's eyes. Sam had to de-escalate the situation, for in the back of his mind, he knew the truth—that the creature inside their patient held all the answers.

"Get the fuck out of my way, Sam! We have to stop him."

"No!"

"You said it yourself—it's that fucking book. He started this, set off some fucking curse upon the world. Why wouldn't you want to stop it?!"

Sam's phone trilled in his pocket. He took it out to see it was his Sara.

"Because it could mean the end of everything," he said. "Of everyone we care about."

Morgan's gaze upon Martin could have killed him on its own. "He got inside your head too, didn't he? Promised you something. Well, I promise you something now, Sam: I'm not gonna let you get between us."

Sam's phone kept ringing.

Morgan barreled into Sam, both of them falling in a tumble to the floor, along with their phones. They rolled and thrashed, Sam desperately trying to keep the syringe at bay. Morgan, driven by his panic, overpowered him and Sam felt the sting of the needle as it pierced his suit and his chest. The effect was instantaneous, his head suddenly swimming.

And ringing.

"It's just a sedative, Sam," Morgan told him as he got up off the floor. "You'll be fine." Then he turned to Martin. "But not this fucker."

Through the murkiness Sam saw Morgan plunge another syringe into Martin's neck and seconds later the man's trembling became convulsions. Jerking so violent that he dropped the tome and toppled to land at Sam's side.

"No, Morgan… Don't—" Sam begged.

And ringing. His daughter calling to him in fear.

His friend scooped up the book from the floor and went to the window. He began ripping pages from the book and tossing them out towards the street below. The pages fluttered in the scarlet air. The all-seeing eye, high above, swelled at the sight—at the betrayal—and exploded with incalculable rage. The earth below it shuddered, then rocked, and Morgan fell out the window, his screams joining the rest of the city's doomed citizens. Sam, his vision swirling, saw the moon split open to release a multitude of tendrils, black and hungry, an invasive, cosmic cell coming to devour and enslave all living things.

Beside Sam, between him and Martin Howard-Phillips, his phone kept ringing out that one final call.

And the first Black Day and Bloody Night ushered in a new age of suffering.

THE FIVE STAGES OF GRIEF

DENIAL

Sam's blood was killing him.

Behind his pale blue eyes, Amy imagined his blood cells at war, devouring each other, depriving him of oxygen, of his very future. On the outside, it was much more evident: the fever, the red pinpricks on his skin, the fatigue, and the nosebleeds. Not a day went by when Sam's shirt or bedclothes weren't flecked with blood.

Blood. Amy was sick of the sight of it. She could only imagine how it felt for her little boy.

They sat in the half-light of Sam's bedroom, Amy perched on his bed with a copy of *20,000 Leagues Under the Sea* in her hands. She thought he'd been quietly listening until he asked her the one question she never wanted to hear him say.

"Am I going to die, Mommy?"

Amy closed the book and looked out the bedroom window. The three-quarter moon hung like a shimmering eye against the velvet night, the soft light dappling through the lace curtains onto the polished wood floor. She contemplated crossing that floor and jumping out the window and into the light when Sam asked his question a second time.

"Mommy, am I going to die?"

"Hmm?" said Amy, not daring to look her son in the eye, focusing instead on the watchful moon.

"What is leu...leukemia?"

"It's when your blood cells don't get along, sweetheart," said

Amy as calmly as she possibly could.

"Is that why I'm tired all the time? And sick?"

"Yes, sweetheart."

"Will I get better?"

Amy glanced down at the cover of Jules Verne's book. She felt like she was the submarine wrapped in the giant tentacles, drowning in the sea—only the ocean was red with Sam's blood.

"Of course you will," she said, standing to tuck him in under the blankets. His sheets smelled lavender fresh, but Amy knew she'd be washing the blood out of them tomorrow.

"So, I'm not going to die, then?"

Amy kissed his forehead. It was cold and clammy. "No, sweetheart. You're not going to die."

Amy went to the door before she could tell any more lies. When she switched off the light, David disappeared into the darkness, which she feared would be what ultimately claimed him.

ANGER

Amy ran a bath, but she let it go cold. She sat naked on the edge of the tub, sobbing, lost in her helplessness. Why would God give her a child, only to take him away? She wiped away the tears and reached for her mobile from the sink. She dialed her mother, who answered on the first ring.

"Amy? Is everything okay? Is Sam okay?"

"Yes, Mom, he's fine. I've just put him to bed."

"How is he doing? Have you checked his blood levels?"

"Yes, yes. He's okay."

"What about you? Are you okay? You sound like you've been crying."

"That's because I have been."

There was a moment's silence before she said: "Oh, Amy. What can I do? Do you need me to come over? I can leave now—"

"No, no, not today. But can you come over in the morning? I have to go to the pharmacy and refill Sam's prescriptions. And I need to get some groceries."

"Of course, love," said Amy's mom. "I'll be there first thing in the morning. Now, are you sure you're alright?"

Amy wrapped a bathrobe around herself. "Sam… He asked me if he was going to die."

"Oh, God." Her mother's voice wavered. "Oh, that poor little boy. What…what did you say back to him?"

Amy looked at her haggard reflection in the mirror. "What else could I do…but lie to him?"

"Oh, Amy. I'm so sorry. It's just…it's just so unfair."

Amy let the water out of the bath and watched it swirl down the drain. "He's never asked me that before. I hope he never asks me again."

Her mother's sniffles came down the line. "Amy, if this is becoming too hard for you… maybe you should consider getting a live-in nurse."

"And how would I pay for that?"

"Well, you can't keep this up on your own."

"I'm his mother."

"No, that's not what I meant, love. Sam's a very sick little boy. He really needs round-the-clock care in a hospital."

Amy gripped the phone tighter in her hand. "The doctors have told me that right now, he's manageable, that he's not in any immediate danger. Frankly, I'm still trying to pay off his last hospital bills." Her mother tried to interrupt. "Look, I called you hoping you could console me, not give me a lecture."

"Amy, I didn't mean—"

"Thanks, Mom. You can forget about coming over tomorrow. I'll call you if I need you."

Amy ended the call. For the next hour, she paced the house, wine glass in hand, wondering if her son would survive the night. She opened a window to stare at the dark, to let in the cold, inviting in anything to quell her sadness. She drank until she was numb and then took herself to bed. As she closed her eyes, she prayed that she could be the one with the murdering blood and not her precious little boy.

BARGAINING

In the middle of the night, Amy awoke to find a shadow standing at the end of the bed.

She sat up and tried to force her eyes to adjust to the dark. Her first thought was that it was Sam, that he'd had a bleed, that the bedsheets needed changing again. But the shadow was far too tall to be her son. Fear swelled in the pit of her gut, and she scuffled back, pressing her back into the bedhead.

"Who are you? What are you doing in my house?"

The shape was still, simply observing her. Amy's heart thrashed as adrenalin pushed all semblance of lethargy from her body. She could taste the fear in the back of her throat. Thoughts raced through her head: who was this intruder, how did he get in, had he hurt Sam, and would he hurt her?

The figure spoke. A resounding echo in the dark. "I heard you, Amy, your invitation."

Before Amy could reply, the shadow leapt onto the bed and pinned her on her back. The man's grip was ice cold, like hardened steel. Then she felt a stinging, biting pain in her neck and the metallic tang of blood assailed her nose. The intruder sucked at her neck, his greedy gulps ringing in her ears.

Blood! He's drinking my blood!

Amy tried to push him away, but he seemed to sap her strength with each mouthful. Her body was ready to return to sleep. She fought the urge. Then, having had his fill, the intruder climbed off her and simply stood beside the bed, like a spent and satisfied lover. Amy saw him smile down at her, flashing blood-streaked fangs.

It can't be, Amy thought. *They're not real! I must be having a nightmare!*

"No," said the man. "You're wide awake."

Amy swallowed, her throat parched, the skin around it throbbing, aching. "W-water..."

The man left the room, and while he was gone, Amy summoned the strength to roll onto her side. If she could reach the bedside table, she could grab her phone. Call the police. *God, I hope he's not hurting Sam.* A moment later, her attacker entered the room so quietly that she didn't notice him until he slipped a hand behind her head and pressed a cold glass of water to her lips.

"Drink," he said.

She gulped the water down, the sound not unlike his just moments before. Amy contemplated smashing the glass across his head, running, grabbing Sam, and getting out to call for help.

"You'd be wasting your time. You're too weak to do anything—I've made sure of that." He took away the glass and carefully placed it on the bedside table. Dazed and debilitated, Amy let her head fall to the pillow. "There's a good girl," he said, pushing a strand of her hair behind her ear.

"Please…" she said. "Don't…hurt my son."

Depleted and in the dark, she couldn't make out his features, but his smile was undeniable.

"He's sound asleep."

A line of warmth trickled from her throat to her left breast. "You…you drank my blood."

"I did," he said, matter-of-factly.

The water started to become heavy in her stomach. "You're a…a—"

"I'm someone who can help you."

Amy swallowed again and the skin on her neck burned. "Help?" What he was saying—how he was acting—didn't make any sense.

He stood and walked to the window. The moon, much higher in the sky now, barely illuminated him. "I overheard your conversation earlier. The way you spoke to your mother was amusing. Still, I suppose looking after an eight-year-old boy with leukemia would be very frustrating for a single mother."

Jesus Christ, how does he know everything about us?

"I can help you help yourself, Amy."

She realized the dizziness was fading, but now her whole body was tingling, her neck especially. She slowly pulled herself up from the bed, one eye on her phone. The man—the creature—seemed not to care.

"What…what do you want?" she said.

He turned to face her. "I've already had what I want." He moved to sit back on the bed, which quickened Amy's heart. "I'm going to give you three choices. You can let me bleed you dry here in your bed, leaving your son an orphan for the remaining few months of his life, you can become my blood slave, or I can put your son out of his misery."

Amy could see the look of glee on his face as hot tears ran down her cheeks. He was reveling in her terror. "No, not my son."

"Think about it. I could end Sam so painlessly. No more leukemia. No more suffering."

She glanced at the bedroom door. The monster's grip was a freezing vice on her thin bones.

"I know what you're thinking. You can't escape, and I'm not going to leave until you make your choice."

Amy grimaced, trying to writhe free. "Fuck you."

He pressed a finger to his lips. "If you wake the boy, I'll kill you both. Now, what is it to be? You die, you become my slave, or I kill Sam. You choose."

Amy imagined him at her throat over and over again, but it didn't compare to the thought of him performing the same vile act on her son.

"So, Sam lives, then?" he said. "Fair enough." He made a move towards her but stopped. "Ah, you have a counter-proposal?"

Trembling, she asked him the question he already knew was coming. "What if...what if you made Sam like you?"

He licked his lips.

"You'd consider that?" he asked.

Amy sat back up and put her hands out to appease him. "I just want him to live...and you can give him that."

"But do you understand what you're asking? You want me to turn your son into a creature that feeds on the blood of the living? Forever. Is that what you really want for Sam?"

She straightened. "I just want you to cure him."

He stood and paced the room. Amy watched him move like he was gliding on nothing but air. Then, releasing a chuckle, he turned to her.

"I see what you're trying to do here."

"I'm not trying to do anything...other than save my son's life."

He waggled a finger. "You're trying to be clever. But you don't realize that I'm the one with the free will here. I'm the one in charge." He considered her for several moments, and Amy wondered if he was just going to kill her then and there and do the same to her son. "No," he said. "I'm not going to do that, but I will make things more interesting. I'll take my previous choices off the table and give you a final alternative."

She wanted this evil gone. Yet, she had to try and save her son.

"Tell me," she said.

DEPRESSION

Curled up in bed, Sam was safe and warm under the blankets, oblivious that his mother was consorting with a creature of darkness. Amy watched him sleep, savoring the steady rise and fall of his chest. He was alive—dying, but alive.

The lethargy and nosebleeds had been the first symptoms to arrive when Sam was just seven. Immediately, Amy had thought the worst, and of course, her motherly instinct had been proven right. Her son would die, and she could do nothing about it. Until now.

"What's it going to be, Amy?" the thing said behind her.

"Why are you doing this?"

"Why? Because it's fun."

Amy sobbed and quickly stifled a cry with her hand. "You're a fucking bastard," she whispered.

He came closer. "I know. Now, enough foreplay—it's time to make your choice."

Flashes of infant Sam in her arms, Sam getting his first tooth, his first day of school, his first nosebleed all came rushing in.

"Oh, that"s all so…saccharine," he said. "Come on. I've made it all so simple for you. Which one of you is going to live forever?"

She stepped closer to her sleeping son. Her duty was to protect him from all dangers—real and now, unreal. She took a deep breath and turned to face her Mephistopheles.

"Turn him," she said.

The creature sneered. "Are you sure?"

Her lips quivered. "I…I can teach him. I can teach him to be better than you. I can give him what he needs so he'll never have to take it himself."

He raised an eyebrow. "So, you'd be willing to become your own son's blood slave?"

"Better his than yours."

He nodded and moved past her in the direction of Sam's bed. Amy looked away, at the blank wall, flat grey in the dimmed light. She waited to hear Sam's cry, his whimper as the monster fed on him. The vile drinking of blood. But there was nothing. Confused, she turned back.

The creature was there, looking at her. She could smell his foul breath.

"You know what?" he said. "I've changed my mind."

ACCEPTANCE

Amy shook Sam awake. His bright blue eyes were wide with uncertainty.

"Mommy?"

It was only her and Sam in the house now, in the dark. Amy sidled up beside him and cradled his head. There were spots of blood on his pillow. She pulled his body heat closer. As she held him, she tried to remember what life was like before Sam fell ill. She failed to recall anything. Anything, except blood.

Blood.

"Mommy, why are you so cold?"

She placed her hand behind his head and craned his neck to the side. Beneath the skin, she could see millions of leukocytes killing their kin. Inside the boy's blood.

"Mommy?"

Blood.

Amy leaned down and kissed Sam goodnight.

TESTAMENT

Journal of Florence Williams, 27ᵗʰ April 1891, 3 p.m.

It pains me to return to my family home, especially when I fear death is waiting for me at the front door.

The letter came only a few days before from a notary named Wickham. It read that my mother, Agatha Deighton, had lost her mind and the will to live, that he needed me to assist in preparing her last will and testament. It would be an arduous and unwelcome task for someone who has not spoken to their mother for almost ten years. Yet, he informed me if I failed to return, the Deighton estate could "fall into wrack and ruin", in his words. My beloved husband, Dr. John Willams, has encouraged me to return home. He says I should see it as an opportunity to reconcile with Agatha, mend old wounds and put our hearts at ease before Mother finally passes on to the Great Beyond. I love John so, but he fails to understand that my mother never had a heart to begin with.

Reluctantly, I left John behind in London and I now ride the train to Yorkshire. With John's surgeon salary I can afford a first-class sleeper car, but strangely I have not been able to sleep. Last night I was plagued with disturbing recollections of the most vivid detail. I fear to write about them here, but perhaps I should see it as an opportunity to exorcise them? The fresh dreams remind me of nightmares past.

One night when I was younger, perhaps eight, or nine, I recall when I was awoken by Mother screaming. I remember walking from my room to her door in the middle of a bleak winter night, holding a candle that barely managed to keep the dark at bay. I remember listening to her screams, too terrified to knock on her door, despite the fact she was suffering. Her cries had become moans, somewhere between agony and ecstasy. I was too young then to understand what the sounds must have been. Yet I know there should have been no one in her room. Mother had been a widow since Father died in the Crimean War. The sound wasn't the expression of loneliness, but something beyond Mother's control. I now know I heard her say "stop!", but being a child, I reconciled her behavior as nothing more than someone in the throes of a nightmare. After all, adults can have nightmares too.

Mother always appeared weakened when I was younger, as if she suffered from some sickness of the soul. She was always tired, which made for an uneventful childhood. She rarely ventured outside. The maids and groundskeepers were left to entertain me. As I never asked Mother why she was always sickly back then, should I ask her about the nightmares when I see her after all these years? Would she even be willing to tell me now that I am older?

The conductor says we are half an hour from the station. I must prepare.

Journal of Florence Williams, 27th April, 1891, 7 p.m.

The following is my account of the evening's events.

Mother is worse than I suspected, but I should have known. The housekeeper, Mrs. Penelope Kolbe, who is still in charge of the general goings-on of the house years after I left, warned me as much.

"Your mother isn't who you remember," Mrs. Kolbe informed me upon arriving. She quickly apologized for speaking out of turn, but I encouraged her to give me as many details as possible.

The house itself was in an acceptable state on the inside, everything polished and clean, the fireplaces immaculate and the parlor domes gleaming, yet the outside was grey and decrepit. There were cracks in the exterior plasterwork, mold, and a creeping vine, which was snaking its way from one corner of the façade to the other. When I requested for work on these unsightly issues, the House Steward, Mr. Bryce Porter, told me plainly that it was "a matter of money" and Porter hoped, with my return, that I was "going to get the family finances in order". I'll admit Mr. Porter raised an eyebrow when I instructed him to arrange for all the exterior works to be undertaken quickly and to pay the workmen in full.

I fear now that the house staff might be under the impression that I am replacing my mother as the head of the household.

While the kitchen maids and under-butlers went about their evening chores, I made my way to the master bedroom in the east wing of the house, where my mother, I am told, spends her days and nights. Of course, meeting my mother after so many years made me nervous, and the fact she was unwell made me even more so, but I was never truly prepared for what eventuated.

As soon as I opened the door, the smell assaulted my senses—a miasma of slow decay. Agatha lay in her bed, eyes closed in silent repose. An oil lamp burning on the bedside dresser illuminated her, and, at that moment, I confess to thinking that she had already gone to heaven until she opened her eyes and cried out in startled fear.

I stepped into the light and soothed her with open hands as she contorted her gaunt face in terror.

"Mama," I said as calmly as I could. "It's your daughter, Florence. Florence Williams."

Agatha Deighton's face was like leather, with the wrinkles and lines of a 100-year-old, not a woman who was only in her sixties. What on earth has happened to my mother in since I have been gone?

The old woman considered me, yet looked right through me. "Florence?" she said.

I approached the bed. "Yes, it's me, Florence."

Agatha turned her gaze to the doors and then back to me. "How did you get in here?"

I frowned. "I came in through the doors, Mama."

"Who let you in my room?" She trembled in fear and confusion.

"Mother, it's alright. I'm meant to be here."

Still, she carried the gaze of someone who did not understand. "Penelope! Penelope, there's someone in my room! Penelope!"

I sat on the edge of the bed, but this only terrified her even more. "Mother, listen! It is I, your daughter, Florence."

She seemed not to hear me, writhing beneath her blankets as if attempting to escape.

My mother does not know who I am.

Journal of Florence Williams, 28th April, 1891, 1.16 a.m.

I write this now with an unsteady hand.

It is the middle of the night, and my mother has been manic, raving.

Her shrieking alerted me a little after midnight, the sound so stark amidst the house's silence that it almost stopped my heart.

I scrambled from the warmth of my old bedroom when I heard it and ran for Agatha's. Mrs. Kolbe's room was on the way, and I pounded on her door to ask for her aid.

Agatha's cries sent my blood cold. It sounded like someone was murdering her. When Mrs. Kolbe reached my side, her visage was my perfect reflection. I tried the door only to find it locked.

"Why is this door locked?" I said to her, confounded.

"We have to keep it locked ma'am, to ensure your mother doesn't wander. Sometimes she walks in her sleep."

Agatha's cries cut through Mrs. Kolbe's words.

"No! No, stay away!"

"Do you have the key?" I begged the bewildered Housekeeper. "We need to open this door, immediately!"

Mrs. Kolbe reached into her robes and retrieved a long brass key. I snatched it from her tremulous hands and unlocked the door.

I find it hard to comprehend, let alone explain, what I beheld there in my mother's room. A shadow, leering in the half-light. A figure, comprised of the very darkness itself, embracing my mother, against her will. I'll never forget the vision as long as I live. Its eyes, which I could feel boring into me, were like twin stars, burning in the night. I stood transfixed, speechless until I heard the House Steward at my back.

"Mrs. Williams? You should not trouble yourself—"

"Candle!" I cried. "Candle!"

Mr. Porter handed me his and I brought it into my mother's

room. The thing—the shadow—retreated into a corner where the light could not touch it.

Then, as mysteriously as it had appeared, it was gone.

I must finish this now and try to sleep, but I fear sleep will only bring nightmares. God, give me strength.

Journal of Florence Williams, 28ᵗʰ April, 1891, 8 a.m.

It is only now, after I have had some rest, that I am composed enough to write.

In the end, it took almost an hour to calm my mother down after the incident. As I sat with Agatha, I kept an eye on the corner of the room, the prospect of the shadow's return lingering like a fog. Now, as I recount this in the light of a new day, I don't honestly know what I witnessed or if, indeed, I saw anything. It was more likely a trick of the light, a figment created by a sleep-deprived mind.

Yet, something was plaguing my mother. Before she eventually fell asleep, she muttered something that chilled my very bones.

"You can't have it!" she'd said to no one. "You can't have my soul."

Eventually, she'd closed her eyes and Mr. Porter, Mrs. Kolbe and I spoke in the hall before retreating to our bedrooms.

"How long has this been going on—these night terrors?"

The Housekeeper and House Steward shared a glance.

"Mrs. Williams, forgive me for saying, but she has always been like this," Mr. Porter said.

"Ever since your father passed, God rest his soul," Mrs. Kolbe added, blessing herself.

"Has a physician been engaged?" I asked them.

"Yes, Mrs. Williams, a doctor came in from town last April and diagnosed her with a deterioration of the mind, and prescribed laudanum to aid with sleep," Porter explained. "He advised that she should be committed."

I scoffed at the suggestion. "My mother needs care, that is certain, but I do not believe she belongs in a sanatorium!"

"Yes, Mrs. Williams," Mrs. Kolbe said, nodding in acquiescence, which only frustrated me.

"You disagree, Mrs. Kolbe? Mr. Porter?" The pair didn't know whether to speak and again each glanced at the other. "You both obviously have a different view. Speak up. Let me hear it."

"Mrs. Williams," Porter said. "I'm not sure what more a doctor could do for Mrs. Deighton."

I pressed a hand to my forehead. "Well, I am unsure how to help her."

Mrs. Kolbe reached out and took my hand. "Mrs. Williams—you did see it, didn't you?"

I looked up at the housekeeper. "See what?"

Again, the silent communication between her and the House Steward.

"The shadow," she said. "You saw it too."

"I...I don't know what you mean..."

Mr. Porter stepped closer. "Forgive us, Mrs. Williams, but I believe you do. I hate to be the one to suggest this, but your mother does not require a doctor, she needs a priest. There's a devil in this house."

10 a.m.

I waited until the staff began their chores before checking on my mother.

She slept soundly—or unsoundly. Which, I couldn't say for sure. How one could shift between sleep and mania I do not know, but this seems to be the sum of Agatha Deighton's life now. As I looked at her and studied the countless lines on her face, I wondered at what point her mind had fractured. Mrs. Kolbe was correct to say that my mother had always been spirited, perhaps aloof, but this was entirely different. Her behavior has all the hallmarks of insanity. Was it my leaving that made her this way? Or was she still grieving my father's death? I now wonder whether I should write to my beloved John and ask him to come to the estate to assess her.

All the unanswered questions and lack of sleep left me feeling drained, yet my mind would not let me rest. As I held vigil with Agatha, I very carefully and quietly examined the contents of her bedside dresser and found inside even more mystery.

I found a photograph of my father in military uniform before he left for the Crimea, his letters of adoration to her, and her Book of Psalms. I opened this book and was about to pray for my mother when I discovered a handwritten scrawl scratched across the printed text and a medal of St. Benedict wedged between the pages. The handwriting was in Latin:

"Vade, Satana! Numquam me temptas tua vanitate.

Quod mihi das, malum est. Venenum bibe te ipsum!"

My Latin is far from polished and, as I sat there attempting to translate it, my mother awoke and recited it, her eyes wide in terror.

"Begone Satan! Never tempt me with your vanities! What you offer me is evil. Drink the poison yourself!"

I quickly reached for her. "Mother?"

She took my hands, displaying much strength for one who appeared so frail.

"Florence! You must leave this place!" Agatha said. "Before he finds you!"

"Mother, what do you mean? There is no one else here."

Her cracked lips quivered. "Don't be here at night! Not at night! He will see you!"

Tears ran down my cheeks. "Mother, please, I don't know what you mean."

"The shadow," she said. "I brought it forth. If it finds you..."

Then she was lost to mental exhaustion before my eyes, simply collapsing back onto her pillows. I wiped away the tears and left her to rest. It wasn't until I was outside her door that I realized I was still clutching the medal of St. Benedict.

1.30 p.m.

After instructing Mrs. Kolbe to watch over Agatha, I wandered the house in trepidation.

I left the first floor, descending the stairs, past the leering portraits of relatives long dead, to the foyer. My heels clacked hard on the marble tiles, echoing around the room. The wind seemed to enter every nook and cranny of the old house, the sound like the hissing of some great serpent. I squeezed the medal in my hand, thinking of the prayer my mother recited from her bed. Why is she trying to ward off evil? What does she mean when she says that she brought the shadow forth?

I think I may have found the answers to these questions. Beyond the kitchens and the staff quarters, deep in the house, lies the cellar. As a child, I never ventured down into its depths out of fear, but now, as a grown woman, I feel it may be where the answers might lie. I will visit it tonight, once everyone is asleep.

7 p.m.

Oh, dear God, I fear my mother is damned! I visited the cellar as I planned and there, amongst the dust and dank darkness, the evil lurks.

In the cold, quiet house, I descended the maintenance hole in the kitchen to the cellar. The wine barrels were stacked along the walls, their circular ends like the countless eyes of some creature observing me in my nocturnal activities. Oil lamp in hand, I scanned every dark crevice of the cellar, and there, in the foulest corner, I saw it.

The shadow!

Two pinpricks of light—the eyes of the thing—considered me. In the dark, the shadow had no definable shape. Only its eyes made me think that it might be human. I was mesmerized by its gaze and I felt fascination, rather than terror, as those two eyes came closer, unblinking.

"Stay away, child!"

The voice was my mother's. She had left her bed and followed me!

"Mama, no! It's not safe to be down here."

I pointed out the shadow to her, but Agatha showed no fear in its presence. She moved past me and stepped between me and the evil. She was so willful and confident, nothing like the bed-ridden, fragile, mindless woman I'd witnessed only hours before.

"Mother, stay back!" I begged her.

She turned her back on the thing to face me, tears streaming down her cheeks.

"I was alone," she said. "When you left, you left me alone in this..."

—she gazed upward—"in this great big empty house. When your father died my heart broke and I...I felt lost without him. You... well, you left, and I knew why. You wanted to be your own woman and I am happy for you, truly. Yet, I was miserable and, in my misery, I did something...ungodly."

The shadow groaned, not with any animal aggression but in melancholy. It shifted closer to Agatha.

"Mother, please move away!" I said, urging her.

"Hush, now child," she told me. "It's alright. "He won't hurt me." ""He?""

The thing crept closer and reached up with its blackened hand to take hold of my mother's.

"I was alone," Agatha said. "And I did something sinful."

I didn't understand what she meant and she must have seen that in my eyes, because she made it clear.

"I went into your father's crypt and I prayed. I prayed for him to return. But my prayers weren't answered by God."

I gazed into the thing's rotted black face, into shadow and bone. It was nothing like my father. Then I looked at my mother.

"You...you are mad," I said.

She snatched the oil lamp from my hand and smiled. "I know. But I loved your father. Just as I have loved you."

I ran from the cellar. I ran through the entire house screaming until every soul was awake. I have forced everyone outside because I fear my mother is about to commit one last mortal sin.

Journal of Florence Williams, 29th April, 1891, 6 a.m.

The Deighton Estate is a charred graveyard. My mother, Agatha Deighton, is amongst the husk of the blackened house, yet I cannot distinguish timber from bone.

Mrs. Kolbe, Mr. Porter and all the staff are safe and as devastated as I, but I have no words of comfort for them, for I do not have any for myself.

I write now from the relative safety of the greenhouse at the rear of my former—now destroyed—home. How I even thought of salvaging my journal in all the chaos, I do not know. Perhaps, subconsciously, I knew I would need a record of the events which have unfolded? Perhaps, more likely, this journal is a testament of my guilt and shame.

I have no inkling of whether the shadow survived the blaze. I pray to God it has gone back to Hell and that my mother is now free and in the tender care of Our Lord. I pray to God that I can return home to my beloved John. That I can forget about this horror and

MARION THINKS HER WORLD IS ENDING

Every waking hour and in her dreams, Marion's thoughts of death and decay were her constant companions. Her mind's eye swarmed with imaginings of school buses full of children colliding on the highway, people choking on their favorite meals, bullets tearing through flesh. On and on. People dying repeatedly until a mountain of bones filled her skull and she screamed at the breakfast table in a desperate bid to let them out.

"Jesus, what was that about?" said her mother, almost dropping her cup of coffee.

"Nothing," Marion said, getting up from the table.

"What do you mean, nothing? You just shrieked like you were having a nightmare—in broad daylight."

"Like you care anyway, Mom."

Marion walked away, leaving the opulent dining room, with its marble benchtops and gleaming silverware, down the hall to her bedroom. Inside were walls plastered with posters of her favorite musicians and bands: Billie Eilish, Anathema, and Type O Negative. She locked the door and pushed in her earphones and tried to let Anathema's grinding guitars drown out the thoughts. Yet it wasn't enough.

A slideshow of children floating face down in swimming pools, of forests consumed by fire and flies crawling over unblinking eyes, rolled through her mind.

The drumbeats in her ears seemed to synchronize with her frantic heart. Through the chaos of music, she heard Diane banging on her bedroom door.

"Marion, are you ready for school? I'm going to be late for the showing over at Riverside."

School? Work? Did social responsibility even matter when you were going insane? One rational thought pushed between the horrors: that what was happening to her wasn't normal, and that she needed to talk to someone about it. Diane should have been that someone, but the woman was only ever interested in her stupid job as a real estate agent and making Marion's absent father pay for his indiscretions.

No, Marion couldn't tell Diane what was going on in her head. She couldn't tell anyone.

The freeway was an endless funeral procession.

Marion stared out the passenger window into the cars beside her. The drivers looked as bored as she felt, trying to get somewhere fast, all the while watching the minutes and seconds pass.

Anathema blasted in her ears with lyrics about not knowing what was behind the skull, and she understood their words all too well. She started to drown in them, letting the music take her away, but a jab in her right arm wrenched her back to reality. She pulled her earphones free and saw a scowl on her mother's face.

"I've been trying to talk to you," Diane said.

"I haven't been listening."

"I know. What's going on with you?"

Marion moved to replace her earphones. "Oh, so you give a shit now?"

"Hey, don't talk to me like that. I'm worried about you."

This time Marion dropped the earphones in her lap and scoffed. "Why? Because it interferes with your precious schedule?"

Diane sighed and let the car creep forward another ten meters before being forced to brake again.

"I'm just trying to talk to you. To see how you're feeling. I mean, you let out a scream at breakfast for no reason."

An unexpected wailing drew Marion's attention and she turned her head back to the window to see a police cruiser tearing up the inside lane, its lights and sirens wailing. On its way to a homicide, or a three-car pile-up, she imagined.

"Maybe I screamed because everything is pointless."

"Everything is pointless?"

"Yeah…"

"You really feel that way?"

The girl gestured to the dozens of vehicles sitting motionless around them. "We're sitting here in a fucking car, barely moving towards nothing but our inevitable demises. We do the same thing every day! I say again: what's the point?"

Diane frowned. "Don't swear, Marion."

"Oh, God! Can we just go back to not talking to each other?"

Marion turned Anathema up and looked back to the road, and for the first time, through all the thoughts of death raging in her head, she wished she was the one who was dead.

The school bell rang inside Marion's head, only adding tension to her residing thoughts. She trudged up the stairs, dodging her classmates' purposeful shoves and judgmental gazes. They looked her up and down, smirking at her dark clothing and pale complexion. She'd endured it all through high school, and she was confident she'd tolerate it for many more days to come.

As soon as she walked through the doors into the school, her eyes met the person she hated most— everybody's favorite stuck-up bitch, Cassie Dixon. Despite her perfect looks, blonde hair, and carefully constructed smile, Cassie's soul was utterly devoid of compassion for anyone who didn't look like her, especially Marion.

"Hey there, *Morticia*. Oh, wow, you really look like death warmed up today." Cassie blocked Marion's escape with her arm. "Maybe you should skip school today and get some sun?"

A cascade of images of Cassie dying, rotting and becoming bones fluttered behind Marion's eyes and a wave of fear washed over her. She pushed Cassie aside and ran down the hall, looking for the closest restroom. Cassie's shrill voice followed her.

"Oh, you'd better run, bitch!"

Marion found a bathroom and ran inside, only to slip on the tiled floor. Her schoolbag struck the mirror, sending shards of glass clacking into the sink and onto the floor. Marion caught sight of herself in the reflection and for a moment, glimpsed someone else standing behind her—a man, smiling in amusement. But he was gone a second later.

Marion blinked and tears flowed. "I'm losing my fucking mind." She found it hard to breathe, the bathroom walls like a vice. Fresh images of blood, screaming mouths, and cracked earth poured into her mind. She clawed at her temples, and the fingertips came away smeared with blood. "Get out of my head!"

She staggered into a stall and dropped onto a toilet seat, desperate to catch her breath. She fumbled for her phone and considered calling her mother, when she realized the screen was also cracked, that she must have fallen against it. She plucked a shard of the screen free with trembling fingers.

"I...can't take this anymore."

The edge of the glass kissed her skin ever so lightly and the subsequent sting shuddered through her whole body. The sensation was invigorating. She pushed down harder, drawing more blood. A long, red line down the inside of her arm.

"Are you in here, bitch?"

Marion started at the sound of Cassie's voice and lifted her feet up onto the lid of the toilet seat, so as not to be seen. As the terror of being discovered set in, so did the realization of what she'd done. Marion pressed her other hand hard against the wound. She didn't want to be found by Cassie—not in this state. Marion's heart beat faster as Cassie walked towards her stall.

Go away, Cassie, she thought. *Go away.*

Marion lifted her hand from her arm and gasped. The wound was gone. There was no sign of blood, like she'd never even tried to slit her wrists.

"I hear you in there, Morticia. Come out or I'll—"

Cassie's sudden scream urged Marion out of the stall and she found the girl on her knees with blood pouring from a long laceration in her left arm, wrist to elbow. They stared wide-eyed at each other, matching visages of terror and confusion.

Marion reached out in an effort to help Cassie, but her blood flowed so unnaturally fast that Marion could only watch as the girl succumbed and collapsed in a heap on the bathroom floor.

Panicked, Marion stepped around the spreading pool of crimson and ran for the door. As she did, she caught another look at herself in the mirror—and she was the one who was smiling.

Once Cassie's body was found, the school was closed and the students sent home. Diane collected Marion and was genuinely concerned, much to her daughter's surprise.

"That's awful what happened to your friend—are you okay?" Diane said on the drive home.

"She wasn't my friend."

"Wasn't she in your class?"

Cassie screamed inside Marion's head, the slits in her arms like writhing red serpents.

"She was a bitch," Marion said.

"Marion! You can't say that about a girl who has just killed herself!"

Marion whirled on her mother. "If you gave one shit about me, you would know that Cassie made my life a living hell every day. I, for one, am glad she's dead!"

Diane's face wavered between concern and pity. "Marion, you don't mean that. You take that back."

The girl watched the traffic. In truth, she was jealous of Cassie—it should have been her wrists slashed, her blood staining the grout between the tiles. Somehow her wish had been given to someone else.

Marion locked her bedroom door and climbed into bed. The thoughts and visions became amplified in the darkened room, like a constant kaleidoscope. The imaginings wouldn't let her sleep; she'd become a slave to them. She lay sobbing between the sheets, skin slick with sweat, heart slamming against her chest.

"Please...please...please...make it stop," she whispered to the dark.

The thoughts answered with bleeding polaroids in her mind: Cassie lying in her pool of blood and her own sneering reflection.

Did that mean she was responsible—or was it the man she'd seen in the mirror?

The sound of flies buzzing filled her ears and, although she couldn't see them in the dark, their tiny legs crawled over her body. She swatted at them, but they kept flying onto and off her, eagerly buzzing and tapping their feet on her lips, her eyelids. Marion shrieked and roiled in the bedclothes, slipping hard to the floor. The flies wanted to taste her tears and smell her breath.

Through the whine of a thousand fly wings, she heard her mother calling. After several moments, the door smashed inwards and the flies vanished, as if her mother's very presence had erased them from existence.

Diane lifted her from the floor. "Oh, Marion, what is going on?"

Marion keened and held her mother tight. "Help me, Mommy... help me."

The white walls of the hospital room should have been a comfort to Marion, but they were a blank canvas for her thoughts.

Diane sat beside her in silent vigil, her gaze constantly on the verge of tears but never quite reaching it. Marion couldn't look at her, so instead, she closed her eyes and tried to focus on more pleasant concepts, childish ones. A soft rabbit in her arms, birthday cake, applying bright red lipstick to her lips. Then a man's voice forced the rare good thoughts away.

"Hello, Marion. It's me, Dr Stanton."

Marion opened her eyes and cried out—he was the man in the mirror! Handsome, in a shirt and tie and white lab coat.

"I'm your treating psychiatrist. Do you remember?"

"No!" Marion skirted towards the bedhead.

Diane reached for her. "Marion, Dr Stanton's here to help you—"

"No! Stay away from me!"

Dr Stanton glanced at Diane. "I expected this might happen." He turned back to Marion and his smile was the same as her smile from the mirror. "Marion, your mother's right—I *am* trying to help you."

"No! Keep away! Keep away!"

Marion was against the wall, like a cornered beast, hissing and spitting. She was pulling the rabbit apart in her mind, the birthday cake was full of worms, and she'd chewed off her lips.

"Don't touch me!"

Dr Stanton called for a nurse. Diane called her daughter's name, finally giving in to the threat of tears. The sharp sting of a needle ushered in a fog of darkness. For the first time in what felt like forever, Marion's thoughts gave her respite.

Marion came to, strapped to a bed with Dr Stanton seated at her side, clipboard in his hand. His voice, however, sounded like it was trying to reach her from the ocean's depths.

"I know you can hear me, Marion," Dr Stanton's voice seeped in, like he was seated on a throne at the center of her skull. "I want you to listen to me. I'm here to help you make sense of your thoughts. That's what you want, isn't it? To know what they mean?"

She nodded, and her brain seemed to slosh inside her head, like she was drunk.

"I know the things you've seen, Marion," Dr Stanton continued.

Her throat was parched but she needed to ask the question:

"Why...why did I see you in the mirror?"

He held her hand. "You don't remember, but you've been coming to see me for some time now."

That didn't make sense to Marion.

Stanton considered his clipboard. "And it appears you've been fighting against my treatments," he said, tone condescending.

Marion's tears were hot on her cheeks.

"But it's alright now. I can help you. Put you back on track."

He smiled, but his face morphed into her own. He was taking control of her mind.

"And when you wake up, all those dark thoughts will finally make sense."

Marion's eyes opened and she was home, safe in her bed. Beams of morning light streamed in through the bedroom window, casting everything in gold. There was not a single horrible thought in her head.

It was going to be a beautiful day.

"It was all a dream," Marion said to herself.

The bedroom door, undamaged, opened wide and Diane walked in, carrying a breakfast tray of toast, a boiled egg, and orange juice.

"Mom?" Marion said, confused, but so pleased to see her.

"Hi, sweetie. I brought you some breakfast. How are you feeling?"

Marion pushed a strand of hair aside. "Um, good, I think. I had the strangest dream."

"Well, you slept like the dead, so that's not surprising." Diane placed the tray on the bed. "Eat up and take your time, okay?"

Marion frowned and looked at her phone on the dresser. It was almost 8am. "Wait, don't you have to take me to school?" She took a bite of toast.

"Oh, no, there's no school for you today. Not after what happened yesterday."

Marion swallowed the toast. "What?"

Diane raised an eyebrow. "What with that poor girl dying I just couldn't let you go back there. Not until you've had some rest."

The toast threatened to come back up Marion's gullet. Cassie's deathly visage flickered inside her head like a switch. On, then off.

"I don't understand—"

Diane clapped her hands together. "Now, hurry up, eat and get dressed." She checked her watch. "Dr Stanton is coming to check on you any minute. Can you believe he doesn't charge for house calls?"

With that, Diane left the room and Marion sat dumbfounded. The unease crept back into her mind. The breakfast tray was so out of place that it shouldn't have even existed.

Marion climbed out of bed and shuffled down the hall. She

could hear her mother talking to someone at the other end of the house.

"Oh, you're already here," she heard Diane say.

Marion reached the living room and found Diane and Dr Stanton in secretive conversation.

"Marion thinks her world is ending," Diane said.

Dr Stanton turned to Marion with a knowing look. "Does she now?"

Deep cuts opened up on Marion's arms, carved by an invisible hand. Blood stained the cashmere rug beneath the girl's feet and spurted onto her mother's high heels. Thousands of flies entered the room through every nook and cranny in the house, like they'd been waiting. The black flies swarmed so thickly they dimmed the light from outside to almost night. Her mother smiled through it all; she seemed blissfully unaware. Then Dr Stanton smiled Marion's smile.

"Don't worry, Marion," he said. "It's all just in your head."

LIKE FATHER, LIKE SON

"**I**t's story time, Daddy," Adam said.

Matt Hansen watched his son from the bedroom doorway and tried to ignore the cold sweat already beginning to form on his back. As the moonlight streamed in from outside the quaint cabin in upstate New York, Adam moved eagerly about the bedroom, putting his toys in the toybox, straightening his diorama of the solar system. Placing the life-sized model human skull on his bookshelf just so.

Eventually, the boy finished buttoning his favorite flannel pajamas—the ones with the astronauts and planets on a dark blue background—turned on his bedside lamp and pulled back the blankets. His toothy smile was wide with glee.

"What story will you tell tonight, Daddy?"

Matt looked down at the clothbound notebook in his hands. It might as well have been a piece of lead. He used to love writing stories. Matt opened the notebook to a page of random words scribbled in one of the corners. Haphazard thoughts in haphazard scrawl. Matt was once a lot more organized with his ideas—when his imagination excited him. Long before he'd taken himself and Adam out to his cabin in the woods, far away from everyone and everything.

"Just a minute…" he told his son, and a scowl crossed the boy's features. Matt's heart quickened, so he quickly added, "please."

Adam's smile returned, and Matt took a breath. He cleared his throat and walked three steps to sit on the edge of his son's bed.

"I'm ready now, Daddy."

There were three words on the page: *Cat, Tree,* and *Snake.* Adam stared at his father and cuddled his scrappy teddy bear close, arms tight around its fluffy neck. Matt coughed nervously again and began to read out loud.

"There once was a boy named Adam, who lived in a cabin in the woods, in Upstate New York…"

The boy chuckled and bounced beneath his covers, the anticipation becoming all too much. A trickle of the cold sweat ran down the curve of Matt's spine.

"Adam had a cat, a sleek black cat…"

Matt braved a glance from the page and noticed Adam had turned to consider the window to the outside world. Beyond the glass, illuminated by the rising full moon, were the branches of an old oak tree. As Matt told his story, a cat, sleek and black, leapt up onto the thickest branch, as if from nowhere. Adam gasped and clapped in astonishment. Matt swallowed hard.

"The cat's name was Samson. He was a proud cat—a cat who believed he was the king of the woods."

Outside, the cat moved and pranced between the branches. Adam clapped more vigorously as his father's tale came to life.

"But the cat wasn't the king of the woods." Matt pinched the bridge of his nose. "In fact, there was another, stronger beast which called the tree home."

A hissing sound crept into the cabin from outside, startling Samson, the cat. The sound only made Adam bounce and clap even more. Matt gulped down the wave of nausea in his gut and read on. He wouldn't stop. Couldn't stop.

"The tree was home to a great big python. It coiled and weaved through the leaves and branches, its yellow eyes adoring Samson the cat. By the time the cat saw the snake…it was too late."

Samson let out a hiss of his own, but it quickly became a howl, guttural and gasping. Matt's son laughed out loud as the snake took hold of Samson, curling and folding its seemingly endless form around the feline until its black fur was lost in loops and loops of shining green scales. Until the cat's cries fell silent.

Matt fought back tears and finished the story: "Sadly, Samson was no match for the snake who was, and always would be…the king of the woods."

He closed the notebook while Adam jumped out of bed and ran to the window.

"Take that, stupid cat!"

The boy's breath fogged the glass, but Matt could still make out the snake slithering back up into the shadows of the tree.

Adam turned to his father in sheer delight. "That was such a scary story, Daddy!"

Matt nodded and pulled back the covers for Adam to climb back in. It took all of Matt's strength to look his son in the eye.

"I can't wait for tomorrow night's story, Daddy. I hope it's even scarier!"

Any other child would be screaming in terror, unable to sleep a wink, but not the son of Matt Hansen. The boy, like his father, had a penchant for the dark things. For terror and horror. Once Adam was settled, Matt backed away from the bed towards the door.

"Don't forget to open the wardrobe, Daddy," Adam added.

Matt shuffled to the wardrobe and opened the double doors wide. There was only darkness within; no clothes, or shoes. Just wood that had been painted black—at the boy's instruction.

"Thank you, Daddy."

Matt turned off the light and the room fell into almost pitch black, save for two burning coal eyes gazing at him from the bed.

"I love you, Daddy."

When Adam was finally asleep, Matt poured himself a scotch and went to his bedroom to cry.

He didn't know how much longer he could keep this up. It had been almost two years on his own with Adam—since he lost Sarah forever. He wiped the tears from his eyes and opened the bedside drawer to retrieve the photo he looked at every night.

He and Sarah, happy.

Before their son came into the world.

"If only I'd known then…" Matt whispered. "Then we could have had a different story."

Matt's tears splashed on the glass of the photo frame. He wiped them away and carried the photo, against his chest, to the window. Above, the moon shone down onto the woods, the tips of countless trees reaching for the stars. The cabin was the only place Matt could think of to keep the world safe from…

What? Just say it.

Matt swallowed hard again.

"I'm sorry, Sarah," Matt said to her photo. "I'm sorry for everything."

His cell phone pinged with a notification:

YOUR PARCEL HAS BEEN DELIVERED

Matt quickly put the photo of his wife back in the drawer and left the bedroom for the front door. He found the courier, a robust man wearing a fluorescent cap and jacket, still on his porch, tapping on a tablet. Matt opened the door, startling the man.

"Oh, hey," the courier said. "Your place was really hard to find."

"Yeah—you have a parcel for me?"

The courier pointed to the large cardboard box on the welcome mat. Matt bent to pick it up.

"So, Harper Collins, huh? You an author or something?"

Matt forced a smile. "Something, yeah."

Realization washed over the courier's chubby face. "Wait a second— You, you're him! You're the guy!"

Matt hefted the box higher, eager to keep his distance as the courier's excitement began to build.

"Yeah, yeah—you're Matt Hansen, horror author! Oh, shit! I love your stories, man. *The Lost Book of Shadows* and…and *My Personal Apocalypse*! Oh man, wait til I tell the guys back at the warehouse. This is awesome!"

Matt turned from him, the "fan-boying" too much to bear.

"Get the fuck off my porch," Matt said, before slamming the door in his face.

The courier's retorts followed Matt as he carried the box down the hall to the back door. Outside, an old oil drum was waiting. Matt lifted the box to throw it into the drum when it slipped from his grip and burst open on the ground. Dozens of copies of *The Lost Book of Shadows* spilled out onto the dewy grass. The book's cover gleamed in the moonlight, enhancing the artwork of a scantily-clad woman, pieces of her flesh being stripped away to flutter in the air like the pages of a book. The sight of it had made Matt proud a long time ago. Now it made him sick.

Matt could never let Adam find out about them.

He scooped up the pile of books and flung them into the drum. He grabbed the nearby container of lighter fluid and doused them, then tossed in a lit match. The books went up in a whoosh of orange flame and Matt savored the wave of heat. The smoky stench of paper and ink clung to the back of his throat.

They can burn in Hell for all I care.

His cell phone rang out into the dark and Matt jumped in fright. Although Matt was outside, he was conscious of waking Adam, so he answered the call.

"Matt, is that you? It's Brian."

Matt grimaced. The last person he wanted to speak to was his agent. "Hi, Brian," Matt said.

"Jesus Christ! I've been trying to reach you for the better part of a month. Where the hell are you?"

Matt watched the flames curl across the books, turning his words to smoke and ash.

"I'm upstate. With Adam. I needed...to get away."

Brian sighed. "Well, I need to see you, Matt—in person. We need to talk about getting you back on the horse."

Matt shook his head and stomped his foot into the ground "I told you, I've given up writing."

"Matt, don't be foolish—"

"I meant what I said!" Matt began to pace.

He moved away from the cabin, fearful Adam might hear his outburst.

"Matt, you realize that you're under contract."

"Are you deaf, Brian? I said I'm done. I'm not writing anymore of that...that shit."

There was a pause on the other end of the line and, for a moment, Matt thought his agent was gone.

"Matt, listen, I know how hard it's been for you. I know what

GREG CHAPMAN

Sarah meant to you, but do you think she'd really want you to throw your life away like this?"

Matt gripped the phone tighter until his fingers began to ache. "What the fuck do you know about loss, Brian? All I ever wanted was her, nothing else mattered to me. Not my fucking books, not even—"

"What about Adam? How are you going to care for him without an income, Matt? Sarah certainly wouldn't want that for her son."

Even with the heat of the flames, Matt could still feel the tears burning his cheeks. He looked to the bedroom window where his son was sleeping. In his mind's eye Matt could see the boy standing over Sarah's body, still clutching the note in his six-year-old hand, the childlike scrawl stark black on white:

I WISH MOMMY WAS DEAD

"Don't call me again, Brian," Matt said.

"Matt, if you breach your contract—"

"I don't fucking care!"

"Have you lost your mind? You're throwing your life down the toilet here, Matt!"

"I swear to God, Brian don't ever call me again—or you'll regret it! Understand!?"

"Is this why you've been buying and burning copies of your books? Oh, yeah, I've heard the rumors, Matt. And let me tell you, if they're true then you really have lost the fucking plot. I know you lost your wife and I'm sorry about that, I truly am. But trust me, you'll lose everything if you keep this up."

Matt threw his phone into the fire, only to instantly regret it. The sparks swarmed into the air, releasing a new swell of amber light and illuminating a figure on the other side. Matt cried out in shock to find his son standing there, watching him.

"Why are you shouting, Daddy?" Adam said, rubbing his eyes.

"Oh, Adam, I'm sorry."

The boy studied his father through the flames. "Why is there a fire going?"

"I was just...just a bit cold. So, I thought I'd light a fire."

Adam's eyes narrowed. "But you've told me that fire is dangerous."

"You...should really go back to bed, son."

"You woke me up. You'll have to tell me another story."

"No. No, Adam." Matt held up his hands in an effort to placate the boy.

"What?" Adam's face carried a ferocity amplified by the firelight.

"I didn't mean—"

"Who were you talking to on the phone, Daddy? I heard you yelling. Something about Mommy."

Matt changed the subject. "Okay, okay. I'll tell you another story. But you have to promise to go back to sleep, alright?"

Matt covered Adam under the blankets and wished he had the courage to use them to smother the child.

He forced a smile instead, eager to hide his true feelings. He had to get the boy back to sleep; he needed time to think, to plan a way to contain his son, or he'd have no other choice but to commit the unthinkable.

"I'm ready for my story now, Daddy."

"Okay, Adam."

Matt grabbed a chair and sat next to Adam's bed. He opened his notebook and while he hadn't prepared anything, he knew exactly what the boy wanted, what he'd always wanted since he could walk and talk.

Fear and terror.

"No, Daddy," Adam said, reaching out to close the notebook. "I want you to read from this one."

From under his blankets Adam produced a copy of *The Lost Book of Shadows*, the woman's shrieking visage embossed and leering off the cover. Matt released an audible gasp.

"Who—where did you get that?"

Adam giggled and turned the book over in his hands, savoring the full wrap-around cover with its splatters of bright red blood.

"I found it on the ground while you were yelling on the phone outside."

Adam hopped up and down on the bed with excitement, yet it made Matt feel like he was trapped in a boat lost at sea.

"Daddy, it has your name on it!" Adam's voice went up an octave. "Did you write this book? Did you?"

Matt grabbed for it, but Adam quickly withdrew.

"It looks really, really scary," the boy said. "You must read it to me!"

"No! No, I am not going to read you that—ever! Now give it here!"

Rage furrowed Adam's brow as Matt took hold of the book. Adam's grip was impossibly strong. Matt tugged and Adam pulled until the book began to tear.

"Let it go, Daddy!" Adam hissed.

"Give it to me!"

Adam released one hand to reach back and grab the ceramic night lamp atop his bedside drawer. Before Matt could react, the boy smashed it across his father's head, plunging his consciousness into the black.

Matt awoke to pain.

His wrists and ankles burning, he craned his neck to discover he was tied to Adam's bed.

"You're really heavy, Daddy." Adam was straddling his chest. The ceiling light cast the boy as a silhouette, dark and menacing.

Matt flinched and began to pull at his restraints. He winced when the ropes tightened, slicing into his skin.

"Adam… What are you doing? You need to untie me."

Adam held up the tattered copy of his father's novel, scowling. "Why didn't you tell me about this story, Daddy? I read some of it while you were sleeping." He smiled then. "It's really scary!"

Matt squirmed on the bed. He had to get free. They were in the middle of nowhere. No one would even hear him if he screamed.

"Adam, please… You don't want to do this to Daddy."

The child flicked through the pages. "Why do the people's shadows kill their owners, Daddy? Is it because they don't like their owners? The people, I mean?"

Matt thought of all the stories he'd ever told Adam; how they'd always seemed to come to life, ever since he was born. Bedtime stories that became living nightmares. And the worst story of all was the first one Adam wrote himself—the five words about his mother.

"Son, listen...you're scaring Daddy and I'd really like you to untie me now."

The boy closed the book. "But isn't that what you do, Daddy—scare people?"

Matt blinked away tears. "They're just stories. I don't hurt people in real life."

Matt saw the realization play across Adam's face and in that moment, Matt thought he glimpsed innocence in his son's eyes. He'd never really meant to hurt his mother back then—had he?

Adam climbed off his father and sat in the chair. "I don't want you keeping secrets from me, Daddy. Not like Mommy did. I want you to tell me the really scary stories—like the one in this book."

"No... I'm not going to do that, Adam."

"Yes, Daddy, you will."

"You evil little shit! You have to stop this now!"

Matt's son picked up his father's notebook. He opened to a blank page and smoothed it down with a swipe of his little hand. Matt pulled on the ropes, but with each pull, they seemed to sap more of his will.

"What if I tell you a story?" Adam said.

Matt's sobs filled the cabin as the boy took up the pen.

"There once was a man who wrote scary stories," Adam said, matter-of-factly, in time with the scratching of the pen. "But he kept this a secret from his little boy." He gave his father a knowing look. "So, one day, the son tied his Daddy to the bed..."

The ropes tightened of their own accord, like the snake in the tree. Adam wrote faster and faster while his father writhed.

"The son made Daddy tell him all the secret stories he could imagine. Because if he didn't, he'd end up just like Mommy!"

Matt cried out in agony as the ropes grew and clenched around his entire body. Adam climbed onto the bed to lay beside him.

"Please don't cry, Daddy. I only want to be like you."

DON'T WATCH

TRANSCRIPT OF VIDEO

PSYCHIATRIC HOSPITAL, KANSAS CITY
Interview room 4, June 24, 1983. 6.02 am

Interview with patient Kansas City Police Detective Russell Dunne and Dr Elouise McGrath.

DETECTIVE DUNNE
My eyes—

DR. McGRATH
Do you know where you are, Detective Dunne?

DETECTIVE DUNNE
(inaudible)

DR. McGRATH
You're in hospital—in the psychiatric ward. Do you know why you're here?

DETECTIVE DUNNE
I—because of—the tape.

DR. McGRATH
Tape? What tape, Detective?

DETECTIVE DUNNE
The one—with the murdered kids—

DR. McGRATH
Detective Dunne, you're not making any sense. Now, I need you to focus and tell me what you remember about the incident at the hospital this morning—

DETECTIVE DUNNE
I—don't want to—

DR. McGRATH
Detective, do you remember what happened in the surgical ward this morning?

DETECTIVE DUNNE
It was the tape—

DR. McGRATH
Detective Dunne. Russell. Can you tell me why you tried to murder a suspect, why you shot your colleagues? Why you hurt yourself?

DETECTIVE DUNNE
Just watch the tape. You'll see.

Dunne sat in his living room, curtains drawn, the television a blinding light upon his despair.

In his left hand, he held the remote. In the other, his Beretta, loaded, the safety on.

On the screen, his daughter Kalie was celebrating her sixth birthday. Kalie's face was illuminated by candlelight, her smile even more dazzling. Behind her stood Dunne's ex-wife, Vivien, when she was happy and still loved him.

"Make a wish, sweetie," Dunne heard himself say to his daughter.

The screen warped and stretched as the VCR tried to auto-adjust tracking on the aging tape. Dunne clenched his hands.

Kalie blew on the candles, four of them went out. Vivien leant in to help the little girl extinguish the other two.

"What'd you wish for, honey?" Dunne's disembodied voice asked.

Thick bands of distortion twisted Kalie's features to breaking point. Dunne pressed STOP before she was lost forever and dropped the remote on the floor. The room plunged into black.

The tears were hot on his cheeks, but Dunne focused on the cold steel still in his grip. He thumbed the safety off. The barrel was a tunnel that would end his pain.

The shrill of the telephone severed Dunne's melancholy. He stared at the phone resting in its cradle on the wall beside the refrigerator. It took him several moments to leave the gun on the armrest and stand to answer it.

The desk sergeant on the other end calmly told him there'd been a homicide at the Rose Hill Cemetery, multiple bodies.

"Is this a joke?"

The desk sergeant assured him it wasn't. "Six college kids making a horror movie. Looks like they succeeded because all but one are dead. The lieutenant wants you there, pronto."

Dunne glanced at his blurred reflection on the TV, his shape fading. "On my way."

Word of the killings must have travelled fast as the TV news crews were already on scene when Dunne arrived. Blue and red police lights clashed with floodlights and camera flashbulbs. Each sweep and burst of brightness was a hammer on the inside of his skull. Beyond the reach of the cameras, shadowy headstones stood to attention inside the graveyard. Sentries to the dead, old and new.

A uniformed officer lifted the yellow crime scene tape for Dunne and he followed the narrow lane to the floodlit crime scene area in the center of the cemetery. Dunne had seen countless victims as a homicide detective, in gutters, the trunks of cars, stairwells, in their beds, and even a bathroom stall. But in a cemetery? There was a first time for everything, after all.

The bodies lay scattered about the area in no discernible

pattern, covered in blood-soaked white sheets. Amidst the carnage, there were several camcorders on the ground, some with their lenses shattered or broken clean off. A boom microphone lay a few yards away, as if someone had thrown it. Headphones slick with someone's blood jutted out from the long grass.

He found the medical examiner—Davidson—peering beneath one of the sheets.

"Dunne, can you believe this? A cemetery."

Dunne crouched down beside him. "Seeing is believing." He rubbed his eyes.

"You feeling OK, Dunne?"

"Uh, yeah. Nothing a cup of coffee won't fix."

"Here, this should wake you up."

Davidson pulled the sheet back to reveal the victim's face. A fair-skinned girl, hair tucked under her pink knitted cap. Her eyes were two bloody caverns, forced inward.

"They were pushed into her skull." Davidson mimicked the act with his thumbs. "Similar injuries to the others. Except for that one guy over there who had his skull smashed on a headstone. They've all got defensive wounds and scratches on their hands and faces. The girl who did this must have been on PCP or something."

Dunne frowned. "A girl did this?"

"Yeah. Paramedics took her to North Kansas Hospital for surgery. She tried to gouge her own eyes out after doing all this. Forensics is trying to gather footage now. If any of it's on tape, then this one will be open and shut, Dunne."

Dunne approached a forensic officer collecting the tapes from the camcorders. Large black Betamax tapes. One had a label with the words GRAVE MISTAKE—Tape #2 written in black magic marker.

Dunne snapped on a pair of latex gloves and picked up one of the cameras. "So, no one's checked to see if any of these still work?"

"From the looks of it, they're probably all broken. We'll have to wait to get the tapes back to the station."

"Right." Dunne turned the camcorder in his hands. He tried the power and it came on with a whir. "Hey…"

Then he pressed PLAY.

He looked through the viewfinder and glimpsed unsteady vision of headstones and a man's terrified face. There was no sound and Dunne realized he'd need headphones if he wanted to hear what had transpired between the call for action and the bloodbath that now laid out around him.

As he watched, the viewfinder flickered in and out, transforming from a bleak cemetery to the candlelit face of a little girl—his little girl.

"Kalie...?" he whispered.

The camcorder slipped from his hands and clattered against a headstone. The noise made everyone turn.

"Jesus, Detective Dunne—what are you doing?" Davidson said.

"Sorry... I thought I saw..."

"Saw what?"

The officers stood surrounded by the headstones, which watched him too.

"Nothing."

Dunne bought a bland cup of coffee from a vending machine at the hospital, but he was eager to try anything to settle his nerves. He told himself he must have imagined what he'd seen in the camera's viewfinder. It was just his rattled mind playing tricks.

He took a sip and savored its heat in his throat. The caffeine managed to reignite his racing mind, though, with thoughts of Kalie, of the murdered teenagers. Eyes driven into their skulls. He tried to shake it off, wondering if he should be on the case—or any case, for that matter. Should a man who'd recently contemplated suicide be investigating a mass murder?

"Detective..."

Dunne tossed his coffee in the nearest trash can as a doctor approached.

"How is she doing? Can I speak to her?"

The doctor adjusted his glasses and hefted the stack of patient files in his arm. "Miss Baker is still a bit groggy from the surgery."

"I just need to ask her a few questions."

The doctor sighed. "The girl has been through a significant amount of physical and psychological trauma—"

"Probably because she murdered her friends."

The doctor stood straighter. "Look, I understand you've got a job to do, but not only is Miss Baker enduring the emotional realization of what happened, she also has to deal with the fact that she is now blind."

Dunne placated him with open hands. "I get it, Doc. I just need ten minutes. Fifteen, tops."

Daphne Baker's hospital room was darkened, almost in recognition of her blindness. The thin, blonde-haired girl lay still in the bed, with her bandaged face turned away from the door. There were bandages on her hands and a single handcuff kept her bound to the bedframe. Where a blind woman would run to, Dunne wasn't sure. After excusing the uniformed officer, he went inside.

"Miss Baker?"

The girl gasped, startled.

"It's OK, Miss Baker," he said. "I'm a police officer. Detective Russell Dunne."

She reached out to him with trembling hands. "I didn't do it! It wasn't me!"

Dunne tried to stay out of her reach. "Miss Baker, please calm down."

"You—you want to take my statement, right?"

"You're ready to tell me what happened?"

"Yes! Yes! I tried to explain it to the officers, but no one would listen to me."

"Miss Baker..."

"Daphne—my name is Daphne."

"Miss Baker, have you been read your rights?"

Even though the bandages covered half her face, Dunne noticed her trembling lips and that she was swallowing hard. There was no denying the guilt she was feeling.

"Yes—yes—when I was arrested."

"Have you requested an attorney? Have you called anyone?"

"My parents—they—they're coming. But I need to tell some-one now. I can't wait."

Dunne retrieved his notebook. "OK, Daphne. I'm listening. Just tell me in your own words what happened."

She reached out again and caught the sleeve of his overcoat.

"No! No, listen! The tape. You have to watch the tape. Then you'll see…"

"The tape? Of the film you were making?"

"No, no—we never filmed anything."

Dunne pried his sleeve free of her grip. "But there was footage. I saw it on one of the cameras—"

"You're not listening to me! The tapes were all blank, but when we got to the cemetery…when we tried to start filming… they were already full with…oh, God it was horrible!"

Dunne stopped writing. "What—you're saying someone had filmed something else on the tapes? How does that explain what happened?"

"There shouldn't have been anything on the tapes—they were brand fucking new! I bought them yesterday!"

Detective Dunne recalled his daughter appearing in the viewfinder of the broken camera out of nowhere. When he looked back to Daphne, he saw bloody tears soaking through her bandages and streaming down her face.

"We shouldn't have watched—" she said. "We shouldn't have watched."

TRANSCRIPT OF VIDEO

PSYCHIATRIC HOSPITAL, KANSAS CITY
Interview room 4, June 24, 1983. 6.12 am

Interview with patient Kansas City Police Detective Russell Dunne and Dr Elouise McGrath.

DR. McGRATH
Can we try and go back to yesterday morning, Detective Dunne— the incident at the hospital?

DUNNE
It's all on the tape—I've told you—

DR. McGRATH
We've reviewed the security tapes at the hospital, Detective Dunne. We saw what happened, but I'd like to hear what led you to attack the other officers.

DUNNE
That's not the tape I'm talking about—

DR. McGRATH
Detective Dunne, why don't we talk about your recent divorce and custody battle. You've been under a significant amount of stress—

DUNNE
You fucking stupid bitch. You have no idea. You need to watch the tape.

DR. McGRATH
You're right, Detective, I don't have any idea. If you could just talk to me. Make me understand—

DUNNE
I don't think you want to understand.

DR. McGRATH
I only want to help you, Detective.

DUNNE
Then watch the fucking tape.

DOCTOR McGRATH
Why? What's on the videotape?

Almost every officer in the precinct gathered around the TV to see the real-life horror show at the Rose Hill Cemetery.

As Davidson unwrapped the tapes from their plastic evidence bags, the crowd whipped into a bevy of excitement. Dunne heard the uniforms whispering, making jokes that the college students' film was more likely "a sex tape gone wrong." Davidson inserted one of the tapes into the VCR and turned on the television. The show was about to begin when the lieutenant strode in.

"Alright, this isn't a damn movie theater—all of you get back to work."

Lieutenant Rodriguez might have been short in stature, but his presence—his authority—was undeniable. He stood, hands on hips, and glared at every uniform as they left the room.

He addressed Dunne and Davidson once they were alone. "Did you get anything from the tapes?"

"We're just about to watch them now, Lieutenant," Davidson said.

"Well, I haven't got all day."

Davidson nodded and pressed PLAY.

Static flooded the TV screen.

"Do you know how to work that thing, Davidson?" Rodriguez said.

"Sorry, sir, there doesn't appear to be anything on the tape."

Dunne walked to the TV, the flickering black-and-white static like a billion swarming flies. "Try fast-forwarding it," he suggested to Davidson.

Davidson fast-forwarded to the end of the tape in a few minutes. Dunne could almost feel the lieutenant's impatience building, like a wave of heat. Davidson tried another cassette, but the result was the same. Nothing but static.

"I thought you said there was footage," Rodriguez said.

"I thought there was too, sir." Davidson glanced at Dunne. "Dunne said he saw something through one of the cameras?"

"What'd you see, Dunne?" Rodriguez said.

"I—nothing, Lieutenant. The Baker girl told me the tapes were blank, brand new when they got to the cemetery. But then—then somehow—they ended up with footage on them that they didn't film."

Rodriguez scoffed. "Sounds like bullshit to me. Get back to

the hospital and talk to her again. The DA wants a confession."

"Yes, sir."

Once Rodriguez left the room, Dunne watched the static, hoping something—anything—would materialize on the screen. Davidson handed him the remote.

"I've got a bunch of evidence to process. Let me know if, by some miracle, you find anything on the tapes."

"Yeah—sure."

The room fell silent, save for the distant chime of desk phones and typewriters. Dunne fast-forwarded through another tape and the next until the static took on a hypnotic quality. He turned the volume up, giving the static a voice—a roar—like rain on a tin roof. When Dunne gestured to press STOP the static wavered, bands of tracking rippling across the screen.

"Wait a minute—"

Beneath the layers of distortion, Dunne made out shadows, figures shifting.

"—what is that?"

The static receded and the figures emerged fully formed. Silhouettes of the college kids, wandering at night between the headstones of Rose Hill Cemetery. Yet the footage didn't make sense because it showed all six of the teens still setting up their equipment. Dunne felt his heart quicken as he realized that someone else had taken the footage, someone off-camera.

Dunne stared at the screen. The camera moved in on the youngsters, creeping closer between headstones and trees. He strained to hear the unknown camera operator's footfalls or their breathing. The only voices were those of the unsuspecting students. The detective almost opened his mouth to warn them when the stranger stopped right at their backs.

The Baker girl was looking through the viewfinder of her camera when she gasped.

"Oh my God!"

"What?" one of the boys said.

"There's something already on my tape."

"What? How? You bought these yesterday, right?"

The camera panned around as the kids huddled in to see what

was on Daphne Baker's screen.

"What the hell? It's us—"

They all turned as one to see who was behind them—and screamed. The students' faces were distorted, eyeless. Exactly how they appeared in death. The screen cut to static. Dunne reached up to press EJECT on the VCR when the screen came alive once more.

His little girl Kalie smiled at him above burning candles. She had no eyes.

"What did you wish for, sweetie?" Dunne heard himself say.

Kalie's voice crackled with static: "That you were dead."

Dunne slammed his palm against the player to make it stop. He pressed EJECT, wrenched the tape free and held it in his trembling hands. The label read GRAVE MISTAKE—Tape #2. The same blank tape that had somehow recorded the demise of five college students, leaving one survivor.

Dunne ran from the room, with the tape in his coat pocket, its images imprinted onto his mind.

The tape slid into Dunne's VCR and whirred to life in the dark of his living room.

Static flooded the television screen and for a moment, Dunne breathed a sigh of relief. What he'd seen at the station hadn't been real.

The picture changed and Dunne watched in cold fear as the tape replayed the killer filming his victims from afar, only to creep up on them from behind. Again, he saw Daphne Baker and her friends screaming from holes in their faces.

Yet it was what followed which had him breaking out into a sweat.

The gruesome footage cut to his little Kalie, her smiling, eyeless face all aglow.

"Why are you watching me again, Daddy?"

He squeezed his tearful eyes shut and pressed STOP on the remote until his thumb burned in pain. Darkness returned to the room.

Sobbing, he scrambled to the phone on the wall and dialed

home for the first time in forever. His ex answered after the sixth agonizing ring.

"H-hello?"

"Vivien? Vivien, is Kalie okay?"

"Russell? Jesus, it's three in the morning—"

"Vivien, please, I need you to check on her. I need to know she's OK."

"Of course she's OK—she's not with you."

The line went dead and Dunne let the receiver fall from his hand to swing and clatter. His cries filled the empty house and he would have kept on screaming, if the tape hadn't come back to life.

Light bloomed from the TV and Dunne dropped to his knees before it. Grainy film of the teenagers being murdered all over again. Decrepit fingers poking into eye sockets. Screams of pain and terror. The final scene showed the same hands cracking one of the boy's skulls onto a headstone, his blood seeping into the name carved onto its mottled surface:

Aiden John Gilmore.

TRANSCRIPT OF VIDEO

PSYCHIATRIC HOSPITAL, KANSAS CITY
Interview room 4, June 24, 1983. 6.31 am

Interview with patient Kansas City Police Detective Russell Dunne and Dr Elouise McGrath.

DR. McGRATH
Who is Aiden Gilmore, Detective?

DETECTIVE DUNNE
You know who he is.

DR. McGRATH
Yes, but I want you to tell me. You believed he was somehow tied to the murder of those teenagers.

DETECTIVE DUNNE
Aiden was on the tape.

DR. McGRATH
You know that's not possible, don't you, Mr. Dunne?

The headstones were stark black against the first light of day when Dunne entered the cemetery for the second time.

He hadn't slept for almost twenty-four hours; his mind wouldn't let him. The images from the tape were shards of glass in his gray matter and he had to get them out. He stumbled between the graves, towards the site where the children had been slaughtered. Then he found it: the headstone the tape needed him to see:

HERE LIES
Aiden John Gilmore
BORN 12/6/1938
DIED 8/8/79

Dunne retrieved his cell, pulled the antenna free and dialed the station. Davidson answered, breathing hard like he'd been running to answer it.

"Dunne—is that you?"

"Davidson, listen—"

"Where in Christ's name have you been? Rodriguez is going apeshit. One of the tapes from the Baker case is missing from evidence."

"I have the tape."

"What?"

Dunne watched a beetle crawl across the headstone. "Davidson, do you know an Aiden John Gilmore?"

"What? Dunne, you need to get your ass back here now. I don't know what's wrong with you, but you can't just leave the station with evidence."

"Gilmore. The name sounds so familiar, but I just can't place it."

"Dunne, you are in serious trouble."

"You know the name, don't you? Aiden John Gilmore."

"Jesus Christ, Dunne. Yeah, yeah, he was a murderer. Mid-seventies. Killed a bunch of people."

"And he was caught?"

"Yeah, yeah—they executed him. Why?"

"Did you know Gilmore is buried right near where the kids were killed?

"What? No. What does this have to do with anything, Dunne?"

"Because Gilmore is on the tape and I think he killed those kids."

"What—"

Dunne ended the call and put the cell back in his pocket. He needed to speak to Daphne Baker again.

Dunne flashed his badge when the nurse refused to wake Daphne Baker at 5.30 am. Shoved a piece of paper in the woman's face and told her it was an arrest warrant. He had to speak to Daphne, ask her why a dead murderer was on the tape. Why he kept seeing Kalie. He was so desperate he drew his gun and pushed his way past. Daphne screamed when he shook her awake.

"Miss Baker, it's Detective Dunne. I need to ask you some more questions."

Daphne gingerly touched the bandages around her eyes. "What? What's going on?"

"What did you see on the camera?"

She sat up in bed, her back against the headboard. "The camera?"

"Yes! The camera! When you and the others looked through the viewfinder, you saw something. That something was filming you."

"Please—I can't talk about this—"

"You saw someone, didn't you! Tell me who it was!"

"I—I don't know—"

"You're lying! You saw him, didn't you? You saw Gilmore! Tell me how he knows about my little girl. Tell me how he knows about Kalie!"

Daphne began to sob, fresh blood oozing through her bandages. "Please, don't—"

Dunne heard a commotion in the hall and he moved to close and lock the door to Daphne's room. Heart pounding, he raised his arm.

"Daphne, I'm pointing a gun at you. I need you to tell me now that you saw Aiden Gilmore."

"Oh, God! Please don't shoot me!"

"Then fucking tell me the truth! You saw him, didn't you? Is he going to kill my Kalie?"

There was banging on the door at Dunne's back. Pleas for him to unlock it and to put down his weapon. To not hurt the girl. He ignored them, instead watching as Daphne Baker reached up with great care to slowly unwrap the bandages from around her eyes.

"You figured it out, did ya?" she said with a man's voice.

Daphne's arm moved faster and faster, the bloody bandages finally slipping free and transforming from cloth to strips of blank Betamax tape. Her eye sockets, once black voids, were now full of TV static. The face of a corpse long dead smiled at Detective Russell Dunne. The face of Aiden John Gilmore.

Dunne screamed and felt his finger squeeze the trigger. He had to stop her—stop him.

Then the door burst in and the room exploded with the sounds of gunfire.

TRANSCRIPT OF VIDEO

PSYCHIATRIC HOSPITAL, KANSAS CITY
Interview room 4, June 24, 1983. 6.40 am

Interview with patient Kansas City Police Detective Russell Dunne and Dr Elouise McGrath.

DR. McGRATH
Mr. Dunne? Mr. Dunne, what made you kill those officers and attempt to kill Ms. Baker?

DETECTIVE DUNNE
(inaudible)

DR. McGRATH
Why did you do that to your eyes? Mr. Dunne?

DETECTIVE DUNNE
(unresponsive)

DR. McGRATH
You thought Ms. Baker was haunted by the tape? That she was possessed by...in your words...a dead serial killer?

DETECTIVE DUNNE
So, you figured it out, did ya?

DR. McGRATH
Detective? Please, you need to leave your bandages on—Oh, my God, what's... What's wrong with your eyes?

END OF TRANSCRIPT

THE YELLOW HOUSE

The road was a black vein, an unstitched wound.

Night was closing in, but Fred was drawn to the yellow of the headlights. The yellow sign. The back and forth of the wipers were like a metronome, but it failed to soothe the one thought inside his head: that he didn't belong in this world.

The three men with him in the Chevrolet paid him no heed. They were nothing more than ushers, he knew, ferrymen. The one to his left wore a yellow necktie. Another sign. Everywhere, the yellow sign.

"Please," Fred broke the silence. "Please don't take me to the bughouse."

The car turned, jostling everyone inside. They refused to acknowledge him, but he had to make them listen.

"You can't..." Fred continued. "You can't let them lock me up..."

Through the windshield Fred saw the entrance to the State Mental Hospital, the gates open wide to receive him. A hungry mouth. The headlights glinted off the iron, momentarily turning black into liquid yellow gold.

"Yellow," Fred said, as he bit his nails.

The yellow flowers on Betty's dress, her yellow hair.

"Betty wouldn't want this—she wouldn't want to lock me up in here!"

The man with the yellow tie put a hand on his shoulder to quiet him. "That's enough, Fred," he said.

"Fred? Fred? Who is Fred? Where is Betty? My yellow Betty?"

The driver shook his head in consternation and braked hard. Through the beams of yellow light, Fred saw the front steps of the hospital.

"Why are the buildings so dark? Why is everything so dark when it should be yellow?"

The engine stopped and the three men climbed out of the car, their faces and bodies obscured by their heavy coats and wide-brimmed hats. The man with the yellow tie took him carefully by the wrist.

"Come on now, Mr. Clayton."

Fred stared at him wide-eyed. "I'm not Mr. Clayton."

Arms took hold of his and pulled him from the car. The air was biting, a thousand burning knives. This world was dark and cold.

"Why won't you people listen to me?"

Fred tried to wrench his arms free, but he was abruptly weakened by the sight of the old man in the lab coat at the top of the hospital stairs. The lab coat was yellow. The man in the lab coat—a doctor—flashed him a smile of yellow teeth. He beckoned Fred with an outstretched hand, his wrinkled index and middle fingers yellowed from years of cigarette smoke. As Fred was taken up the stairs he got a closer look at the hospital's façade—painted bright yellow. Fred cracked a smile of his own.

"Is this the place?" he said. "The yellow house? Is this the temple?"

The three men escorting Fred exchanged worried glances, but the doctor's voice quickly assuaged their fears.

"Thank you, gentlemen, I'll take it from here."

The doctor took Fred by the elbow and led him towards the front doors.

"Welcome, Mr. Clayton, my name is Dr. Burke. We're going to take good care of you."

The old man's eyes, above his half-moon spectacles, seemed to have a calming effect.

"Is this...the yellow temple?"

Dr. Burke smirked. "Come on, let's get you inside. There's a great deal to discuss."

They bathed him with yellow soap which smelled like dandelions and dressed him in a yellow shirt and dark overalls. Already Fred felt at home, the yellow signs comforting and orderly. Perhaps he'd been wrong? Perhaps this was the place he'd always meant to be?

A nurse in a yellow hat and uniform took his blood and offered him water from a yellow cup. He hardly felt the needlestick because she reminded him so much of his Betty. Betty all in yellow.

"Is this place the Yellow Temple?"

The nurse looked up briefly from her work, but she didn't reply, only offered him that same knowing smile. What needed to be said? The truth was all around him. He belonged here. With others just like him.

After drawing his blood, the nurse walked Fred from his room down the hall, where Dr. Burke and other nurses and men in yellow lab coats were seated, patiently waiting for his arrival. The nurse sat Fred at the front of the room, and he stared back at them. Then Dr. Burke stood to speak.

"Good evening, gentlemen, I'd like to introduce you to our newest patient, Mr. Fred Clayton."

Fred tried to smile at the audience, but none of them smiled back. Many of them smoked cigarettes, the haze, which was yellow, hovering thickly above them.

"Mr. Clayton is a 44-year-old married man, with no children. He has been an automotive mechanic for 25 years and until recently, was in a good state of mental and physical health. Two nights ago, Mr. Clayton attacked his wife of 12 years. The attack was entirely unprovoked. When Mr. Clayton was arrested, he told the officers that he beat his wife because she'd dyed her hair. Mrs. Clayton is a natural blonde, but she wanted to be a brunette." Burke turned to look at Fred in that moment, but there was no warmth on this occasion, only judgement. "This, in itself, should not have instigated such violence, but according to Mrs. Clayton it was the climax of a series of strange events concerning her husband."

Fred listened to Dr. Burke intensely.

"In the week leading up to this event, Mr. Clayton had begun experiencing what I believe to be the onset of paranoid schizophrenia. A delusion centered on the color yellow. Right now, he believes he sees the color yellow, even in the lab coat I am wearing, and in the nurses' uniforms."

Burke opened a manilla folder and produced a tattered and yellowed book. Fred gasped at the sight of it, drawing the gazes of the onlookers. Burke waved it near Fred, who followed it with slow motions of his head, like a dog would a piece of raw meat.

"As you can see, the book seems to still have some sort of hold over him, as does the color yellow."

"What is the title of the book?" one of the doctor's asked.

"The King in Yellow," Burke replied.

Fred smiled as the intonation touched his ears. "Yellow," he said.

Burke continued. "It's believed that Mr. Clayton found this book under the passenger seat of a car he was restoring in his garage. Although Mr. Clayton is not an avid reader, his wife told the judge at the committal hearing that her husband became obsessed with it, reading it repeatedly, morning, noon and night."

"Dr. Burke?" another doctor said. "The book—*The King in Yellow* —what is it about?"

Burke shrugged. "I haven't the faintest. But it's a play, not a novel." Burke handed the book to his colleagues and they began scrutinizing it. "Now, perhaps we can ask Mr. Clayton some questions in an effort to ascertain the extent of his delusion. Would you mind obliging us, Mr. Clayton?"

Fred nodded, but kept his eyes locked on the book as it was passed from one doctor to another.

"Splendid. Mr. Clayton, why do you think you're in hospital?"

The doctors flicked through the pages. Would they see it too, he wondered.

"Be…because this is where I belong. Not out there."

"You feel you belong here?"

Fred looked at Dr. Burke as if for the first time. "Don't you? Isn't that why you wear the yellow coat?" He turned to the others. "Why you all do?"

Burke addressed his staff. "The delusion is so fully formed that Mr. Clayton can actually see it in others. He believes that his wife changed her hair because she was trying to deny herself from some sort of hidden truth. An alternate reality. Right now, he believes that we're all in on the charade. A conspiracy of color, if you will."

Some of the doctors chuckled and whispered, their eyes probing Fred with that same look Betty gave him: that he was a fool.

"You…you don't believe me?"

Dr. Burke placed a hand on Fred's shoulder. "We believe that we can help you Mr. Clayton. That we can release you from these shackles." He took the book back from one of his colleagues. "This book holds no power over you. It is a fiction and nothing more." He flicked through the pages. "There is no King in Yellow, no Carcosa—"

Fred felt himself go rigid as words escaped his mouth all on their own: "'One morning early in May I stood before the steel safe in my bedroom, trying on the golden jeweled crown. The diamonds flashed fire as I turned to the mirror, and the heavy beaten gold burned like a halo about my head. I remembered Camilla's agonized scream and the awful words echoing through the dim streets of Carcosa.'"

Dr. Burke recoiled. "Remarkable. His voice has changed, in tone and inflection. Nurse, I believe we should take Mr. Clayton back to his room at once."

Fred went limp in the nurse's arms and she had to call for a wheelchair. As they wheeled him away, the room buzzed with chatter, the doctors all mingling around their leader, eager to get another glimpse at the book.

"Gentleman, I believe that our course of treatment for Mr. Clayton is clear—we'll commence insulin shock therapy in the morning."

As the hallway became a blur, Fred realized that the only way Dr. Burke and the others would truly understand was if he showed them.

The next morning there was no shower, or breakfast. There was a distinct lack of birdsong. As if they could sense Fred's trepidation. After taking more of his blood, Dr. Burke and six nurses escorted Fred to a room at the end of the hall. It was still dark and the other patients slept soundly in their beds. In the dark, Fred could barely make out the yellow of the doctor's coat and this troubled him.

"Where are we going?" Fred asked.

At the head of the entourage, Dr Burke strode with the confidence of a soldier on the march. Fred noticed he clutched the yellow book in his right hand.

"My…my book?" Fred muttered. "You've still got my book."

The good doctor looked back over his shoulder. "I've been reading it, Mr. Clayton, in an attempt to understand your delusion. It's most fascinating."

"Yes…it is."

The double doors opened onto an operating theatre style room. A stretcher sat in the center and the walls and floors were tiled. Yellow tiles framed by grout as black as night. No one but Fred seemed to notice the significance of the yellow tiles. The nurses had him lie on the bed and remain still as they fastened thick leather straps around his wrists, chest, and ankles. Then they pricked his arms with needles. Intravenous tubes dangled about in the air like snakes. The way the nurses moved with such purpose should have given Fred comfort, but he knew not one of them would truly be able to help him until they helped themselves.

"Is the insulin ready, Nurse?" Burke said.

"Yes, Doctor," she replied.

"Good, then let's begin."

Burke leaned in close to Fred. His breath smelled of cigarettes. "Now, Mr. Clayton, we're going to administer the insulin. It will make you feel very sleepy. The injections will provoke seizures and it's these seizures which will help your mind rail against the delusions you've been experiencing. Do you understand?"

Fred blinked. "Will I be a sacrifice, Doctor?"

Burke turned to one of the nurses. "We'll start with 100 units, Nurse, and increase the dosage by 50 units per hour." Then he placed a hand on Fred's shoulder. "We're here to make you well again, Mr. Clayton. Don't you want to be well?"

"Don't you want to know the truth?" Fred whispered back. "You've already read about it."

Burke turned away and nodded to the nurse, who turned a dial on one of the intravenous tubes. Fred shivered as a coldness spread along his arm and over his chest, like he was adrift in an icy sea. He craved warmth, the golden heat of a Carcosan sky.

Instead, darkness claimed him.

Fred was taken into the arms of a golden light. Its caress was like a summer stream and he was a leaf carried by its current. He laid back; the bed he'd been placed upon in the hospital was gone, at least from this world. Voices called to him and when he turned to hear them, he found he was not alone.

Dr. Burke and his staff had been replaced by figures in golden robes. The beings had no faces beneath their hoods, only caverns of the deepest, darkest black. Yet Fred knew they could see him— no, could see into him.

"Mr. Clayton?" one of them said, but Fred couldn't be sure which.

"I knew it was true," Fred said, smiling with blessed relief.

"Mr. Clayton." This time the voice came from the right, not from inside his head.

The gilded shape leaned in, so close that Fred could see that its robes weren't fabric at all, but rather liquid, shifting and twisting to maintain its shape. Over its shoulder, Fred glimpsed twin suns beating down upon a withered city.

"Our words are your words, Mr. Clayton."

"Yes." Fred could taste the salt of his tears.

The creature's robe sprouted a tendril, which became an arm and then a hand. In its fingertips sat a crown. The crown slipped onto Fred's head, like the warmth of a lover. The figure spoke one last time:

"Then make them theirs."

Dr. Burke took Fred Clayton's wrist to check his pulse. Alarmingly, it was well over 120 beats a minute. The doctor checked the insulin flow and listened to his patient's heart. The rhythm was normal, only on the verge of being tachycardic. He would have to keep a close eye on this man and be prepared to pull him from his coma quickly if need be. Burke glanced over at the electroshock machine nearby. If the insulin shock therapy didn't take, then he'd have to resort to stimulation of a more direct kind.

Burke took a seat next to Clayton and studied the book that had apparently sent the average everyday motor mechanic on a rapid downward spiral.

The King in Yellow was a strange text, a series of interconnected plays which hinted at another reality. How a work of fiction had altered Mr. Clayton's psychological state he wasn't sure. Perhaps the man had already had deep-seated schizophrenic tendencies? These normally presented themselves in the young, but mental illness was, by its very nature, unpredictable. There was still so much that was unknown. Burke puffed on his cigarette. There was a clear irony between the science of psychology and the power of story, as both stemmed from a desire to understand the human mind.

A gentle touch to his shoulder startled him, and he turned to find a nurse at his side.

"Excuse me, Doctor, but Mr. Clayton's wife is here. She was hoping to see her husband."

Burke frowned. "Had no one informed her that her husband is currently undergoing treatment?"

"I'm sorry, sir. I tried to explain but she said if she couldn't see her husband then she wanted to speak with you."

Burke nodded, stubbed out his cigarette and slipped *The King in Yellow* into his lab coat pocket. For some strange reason, it gave him comfort to know it was there.

The good doctor thought it oddly provocative that Betty Clayton chose to wear a yellow dress, especially given the fact that her husband's violent action was evident on her face.

She held out her hand and Burke took it, trying his best to

offer a reassuring smile.

"Hello, Mrs. Clayton. I apologize, but we weren't expecting you," he said.

Betty teased a lock of yellow hair behind her ear. The hair gleamed against the purple bruises on her face and neck. "I'm sorry, Doctor," she said. "I just really needed to see Fred."

Burke gently patted her hand. "I understand. Unfortunately, Mr. Clayton is in the middle of his treatment."

"The...insulin therapy?"

"Yes, that's right. So, the nurses did explain, then?"

"Mm-hmm. They said he'd be sleeping."

"In a coma...but he is perfectly fine. We're monitoring him constantly."

Betty swallowed. "I thought insulin was for people with diabetes. Wouldn't this be like...poison?"

Burke cleared his throat. "Well, it shocks the system back into normality. Like a reset."

"And it works?"

"The majority of the time, yes. Now, Mrs. Clayton, I am very sorry, but I'm afraid your visit falls just outside the normal visiting hours—

"Can I see him?"

"Mrs. Clayton—"

"Please, you said it yourself, he's in a coma. I just...want to tell him I forgive him. It will only take a few minutes."

Burke could see the sincerity in her blackened eyes. Despite everything, she had an inner strength.

"It's rather unorthodox, but... Yes, of course. Just a few minutes."

To Dr. Burke, Betty Clayton resembled a widow standing beside her comatose husband. The only thing at odds with the scene was that she was not wearing black. Yet, the manner in which she carried herself gave the psychiatrist pause. She did not seem fearful or anxious. He watched as she took her husband's hand and stroked it.

"Is he in pain?" she said.

Burke stepped closer, careful not to intrude. "No, he would be feeling absolutely nothing."

She stroked Fred's brow with delicate fingers. "I imagine he is dreaming."

"Inducing a coma allows the mind to heal. There are no signs of the normal sleep-wakefulness cycle, so it's highly unlikely Mr. Clayton is dreaming."

The stroking became more insistent, as if she were tracing a shape on his forehead. Dr. Burke frowned.

"Mrs. Clayton, how are you feeling…after the ordeal?"

"I've missed Fred immensely. It's so good to see him again."

"Yes, I suspect it's heartening to see him…in a much calmer state. Especially after what happened."

She smiled and ran her fingers through Fred's hair. "It was meant to be."

Dr. Burke shifted to try and get a better look at her face. There was something off-putting in her gaze. A perverse lust.

"You…must have been in fear of your life."

"Oh, not at all," she said. "It was just a shock to his system."

"What do you mean?"

This time she turned away from Fred to look at him. "The book."

Dr. Burke could feel the weight of it in his lab coat. "The book?"

Betty moved to him and slid her hand into his coat to retrieve it. "This book. I was

reading it to Fred when he finally woke."

Burke's throat tightened. "You? You were…reading it to him?"

She opened the book and flicked through the pages. "Of course. I was the one who hid it in that car for him to find."

"You told…the police that he just attacked you… I…I don't understand."

Betty smiled and for the first time Dr. Burke noticed her eyes were golden, like two miniature suns housed inside her skull. She leaned over her husband and whispered in his ear and immediately the man sat up, breaking his leather straps. His eyes wide open. Burke was paralyzed by confusion and fear. He could only stare as

Fred Clayton plucked the insulin catheters from his arms, walked to the electroshock machine, and took hold of the paddles.

"I...I...don't understand..." Burke said again.

Betty stood aside as her husband came at the psychiatrist, the harsh buzz of the device echoing inside the room.

"Oh, don't you worry," she said. "We'll see that you do."

Dr Burke awoke to the sounds of screams. He tasted blood and wool in his mouth and quickly realized he'd been bound and gagged. As his eyes adjusted, it became evident the screams were coming from his fellow psychiatrists and the nurses. They were all being subjected to horrible violence at the hands of the people who had once depended upon them for care.

The patients ran about the hall, barely clothed, slathered in blood. Several, Dr. Burke saw, were huddled in a corner, urinating on one of the doctors, staining his coat. As he howled the patients chanted the word "yellow," over and over.

A makeshift stage had been assembled with the tables and chairs from the cafeteria and recreational room. Atop it stood Fred and Betty Clayton, hand in hand, smiling down on the melee unfolding below. The pair had fastened crowns made of bed springs around their heads. Betty came forward to address her parishioners. In her left hand she held the book that had started it all.

"This is the King in Yellow..." Betty told the gathering.

Fred Clayton's eyes began to exude a blazing light and Betty praised him with a rousing cry:

"And I am his queen!"

Behind them Dr Burke beheld the dawn of a new day. Twin suns rising to herald an age of madness. The King and Queen in their Yellow House.

Betty opened the book and began to read from the First Act:

> *Along the shore the cloud waves break,*
> *The twin suns sink behind the lake,*
> *The shadows lengthen*
> *In Carcosa.*

Strange is the night where black stars rise,
And strange moons circle through the skies,
But stranger still is
Lost Carcosa.

Songs that the Hyades shall sing,
Where flap the tatters of the King,
Must die unheard in
Dim Carcosa.

Song of my soul, my voice is dead,
Die thou, unsung, as tears unshed
Shall dry and die in
Lost Carcosa.

TORMENT

Prologue

Boston, Massachusetts, May 7th, 1984

Felicity's teeth were bloody from gnashing her skin raw from her own fingernails, but even when she spat and wailed in his face, the deacon refused to relent.

Resigned to his task, he tied the leather bonds around her hands and feet and let only the word of God enter his mind; God would set them both free. Suddenly the thing the deacon knew was inside Felicity ceased its howling and sprouted false tears from her eyes.

"Why are you doing this to me?" Felicity's demon said.

The minister sprinkled Felicity with holy water, sending her into a new fit of rage.

"Douglas! Answer me!"

Deacon Douglas Mackinnon blessed himself and opened his Bible. His words soared above Felicity's pleas.

"Let us pray. God, whose nature is ever merciful and forgiving, accept our prayer that this servant of yours, bound by the fetters of sin, may be pardoned by your loving kindness."

"Douglas! Stop it!"

Douglas read on. "Holy Lord, Almighty Father, everlasting God and Father of our Lord Jesus Christ, who once and for all consigned that fallen and apostate tyrant to the flames of Hell, who sent your only-begotten Son into the world to crush that roaring lion; hasten to our call for help and snatch from ruination and from the clutches of the noonday devil…"

Felicity reared up in the bed and the bonds around her wrists creaked from the pressure.

"Douglas, you have to let me go…I'm sick!"

Douglas looked at her for an instant and rejected her demon's lies.

"…this human being made in your image and likeness. Strike terror, Lord, into the beast now laying waste to your vineyard…"

"There is no demon in me!" Felicity screamed. "Douglas, please stop!"

"…fill your servants with courage to fight manfully against that reprobate dragon, lest those who put their trust in you and say with Pharaoh of old: 'I know not God, nor will I set Israel free…'"

Felicity wailed again, a great curdling shriek.

"Let me go! Let me go! You can't do this to me!" She writhed and pulled, but Douglas had tied the bonds tight. Welts had begun to surface on the skin of Felicity's wrists.

Douglas continued to seek strength from the Word.

"Let your mighty hand cast him out of your servant, Felicity, so he may no longer hold her captive, whom it pleased you to make in your image and to redeem through your Son; who lives and reigns with you, in the unity of the Holy Spirit, God, forever and ever. Amen."

Felicity's eyes were wide with pain and fear.

"Let me go or I'm going to kill you, you fucking pathetic piece of shit! You think you know what you're doing? You have no fucking clue. You never have! You have never wanted to help me!"

Douglas pointed a crucifix at her.

"That won't help me," she exclaimed.

"I command you, unclean spirit, whoever you are, along with all your minions now attacking this servant of God, by the mysteries of the incarnation, passion, resurrection and ascension of our Lord Jesus Christ, by the descent of the Holy Spirit, by the coming of our Lord for Judgment, that you tell me by some sign, your name and the day and the hour of your departure.

"I command you, moreover, to obey me to the letter, I who am a minister of God, despite my unworthiness; nor shall you be emboldened to harm in any way this creature of God or any of their possessions."

Felicity's screams flowed out of the room into the hall. There, cowering in the doorway to her room, her hands clasped over her ears, was nine-year-old Jessica. She had never heard her mother so scared before either and this knowledge made her tremble.

No matter how hard she squeezed her hands to her ears, Jessica still heard her mother's screams and the deacon's tirade. Jessica had listened to it for years, but the din was at its very worst over the past few hours.

The deacon shouted at the demon to leave her mother over and over. Jessica didn't know what a demon was, but she knew there was something wrong with her mother, there always had been. The doctors couldn't help her. Jessica prayed the deacon would find the cause; all she wanted was to have her mother back.

Suddenly, the screaming stopped.

Jessica was overwhelmed by the silence. She pulled her hands away from her ears and listened to the lock in her mother's bedroom door turn. The deacon appeared, looking spent, his eyes red from tears.

"Is Mommy okay, Daddy?" Jessica asked the deacon. Douglas MacKinnon crouched down and held his daughter's hand. She could smell his sweat. Behind him, Jessica saw her mother's face, blanched and frozen in terror, her tongue bulging between her teeth.

The deacon touched Jessica's cheek, tearing her gaze away from her mother's face.

"She's with God now, Jess," he told her. "She's at peace."

Part One

Twenty-five years later

Trepidation twisted knots in Jessica Newman's stomach as she drove up to the gate outside her father's old home in Aviemore, Scotland.

She was thousands of miles from home and literally standing at the doorway to a past she didn't want to resurrect. However, fate had intervened.

Jessica's happy existence with her husband and teenage son in Boston had been shattered a month before when a solicitor, representing the estate of Douglas Mackinnon, contacted her with the news of his death.

It was the first time she'd heard his name spoken aloud in more than twenty years.

The solicitor told Jessica her father's death was declared a suicide. He was found dead in his ancestral home, located in the secluded hills of north-east Scotland, a single gunshot wound to his head. He'd moved back to Aviemore after the court case to hide alone and die alone.

With the news came a long period of grief for Jessica. Old fears and emotions about her mother and her last dreadful night on Earth came rushing back to the surface, and nothing could shut them out.

Jessica told the solicitor she wasn't interested in her father, that he'd been dead to her for a long time. But there was the matter of the Mackinnon home: her father had left it to his only child in his will. She had to decide what to do with it.

In the nights that followed the solicitor's dark news, Jessica was plagued with nightmares of her mother crying out for help as her father loomed over her like a devil. The dreams—the same ones every night—were vivid, and the irony of her parents' roles being reversed was troubling.

As far as Jessica, the Catholic Church and the Courts were concerned, Felicity Mackinnon had not been possessed by a demon on the night she died.

Douglas Mackinnon, an ordained deacon, was found to have been desperate, but not criminally negligent, when he chose to perform an exorcism on his wife on the night of May 7, 1984.

Jessica could almost hear the Judge's closing remarks to the jury twenty-five years ago, as if he stood behind her reciting it for a second time. He ruled that, as a devout man of the cloth, Deacon Mackinnon felt lost, and seeking help from his church and his God, did the only thing he felt he could do at the cost of his wife's life.

During the three-week trial, Jessica heard her mother exhibited the symptoms of a form of manic-depressive disorder; unpredictable mood swings, suicidal tendencies and a prevalence towards self-harm. Deacon Mackinnon, Felicity's husband of fifteen years, however, did not believe her condition was at all psychological.

The good deacon, the defense said, had served his church for twenty years at the time of the exorcism and was regarded by his fellow clergymen and parishioners as "the thirteenth apostle".

As a family man, Deacon Mackinnon had no equal, his friends testified. These friends had no clue of what went on behind the doors of the deacon's gable home in South Boston. Jessica knew, all too well. Her childhood, her entire life, was defined by the horrible actions of her parents. She carried the memories like a cancer in her soul.

Even now, all these years later, Jessica could remember when her mother ventured into her room one moonless night, the gleam of steel in her hand. Her little girl screams still echoed inside her to this day. She could almost see her father's solemn face as he dragged her mother away and locked her inside the master bedroom, never to appear alive again. With practiced thought, Jessica could block the psychic pain out, but she knew her resolve was about to be tested.

The details of the exorcism ritual Douglas tried to perform on May 7, 1984 played out in graphic detail through Jessica's eyewitness testimony. Jessica recounted how she'd heard her mother begging her father to let her go and how the clergyman simply ignored her.

A psychiatrist interpreted Jessica's evidence as proof of Felicity's fractured psyche; that in an effort to save herself Felicity tumbled deeper into her mania and became violent and dangerous, but not demonic.

Deacon Douglas Mackinnon declined to take the witness stand.

The jury agonized on the verdict for three days, until they ultimately found him not guilty of criminal neglect.

The damage of the trial was too much for the Catholic Church and Douglas Mackinnon was subsequently defrocked. It may not have been as final as prison, but the public and the media accepted the punishment still carried considerable impact.

Jessica, who was then in the care of her mother's parents following Felicity's death, was later informed her father had fled back to his home country.

Now, more than two decades on, Jessica stared at the decrepit place her father had escaped to. The house, a crumbling manor, looked as dark as Deacon Mackinnon's past. Jessica felt it exuded fear. The voice of Jessica's son, Alex, broke the long silence.

"What a dump!" he exclaimed.

"Alex, please," Jessica scolded him as she parked the rental car outside Mackinnon Manor. Still, she found it hard not to agree with him. The paint was peeling, the shutters cracked and the wood rot so extensive the entire house looked as if it were infected with some debilitating disease.

"Your father lived here?" Jessica's husband David asked.

"That's what the solicitor said," she replied as she turned off the ignition and stepped out into the chilly October morning air. Green dales, shrouded in a distant fog from the Grampian Mountains, only accentuated the manor's menacing appearance. Jessica checked the address against the map. "This is definitely it," she added, disappointment evident in her voice.

"Looks like it's been this way for years," David said. He scanned the structure and pursed his lips, as if he'd swallowed something distasteful.

Jessica held his hand as anxiety gripped her again. David was a good man; he'd been her rock throughout the whole ordeal. He'd shown only compassion when she'd revealed the sordid secrets of her childhood. He'd never felt betrayed when she'd finally told him. He understood, which only strengthened Jessica's love for him.

David looked toward her with his steely blue eyes, the icy wind tousling his scruffy black hair. "You sure you want to do this, Jess? It's not too late to turn back."

Jessica pulled her coat tightly around her, but she knew it wasn't really the cold that bothered her. She tucked her long, wavy brown hair out of her brown eyes and flashed David a half-smile.

"I don't know," she said. "I'm not sure I want to be here, but at the same time, I want answers, you know?"

David hugged her. He felt warm: her warm guardian whose love brought her out of the darkness all those years ago, when she was a thin twenty-something, overwhelmed with grief and depression, trying to study at college. He had been her protector ever since.

"It's your choice, Hon," he told her. "Whatever you want to do, I'm with you, okay?"

"Thanks," she said and stood on her tiptoes to kiss him.

Alex's sigh was audible above the Highland wind. They turned to watch him kick over a rusting tin bucket in the long grass. Jessica understood his frustration; Alex didn't want to be here and she wasn't sure she did either, but it was the only way Jessica knew she would attain closure.

Alex was at the sensitive age where peer pressure and outward impressions meant everything. Jessica knew his dark clothing and the scraggly, shoulder-length black hair that obscured his green eyes put him squarely in the "EMO" crowd, those pre-pubescent teenagers who willingly regarded themselves as outsiders, listened to morbid punk rock music, wore black and acted constantly depressed. Jessica hoped it was only a phase he would eventually grow out of. Still, she knew her son would not consider living in a dilapidated house in the Scottish countryside very "cool".

Jessica ascended the rotting stairs and stopped to examine the front door. Its brass doorknob looked like it had been turned a million times. A roll of thunder echoed over the house and the boards under Jessica's feet shuddered in response. Her heart quickened its pace, but her husband's voice brought her back from the brink of fear.

"Someone's here," he said, pointing to a four-wheel-drive coming up the path towards the manor.

Jessica turned away from the door, grateful for the distraction. They all watched as a short, thin, balding man in an expensive suit stepped out from the vehicle and flashed the family a shining smile.

"You must be the Newman family," the man said with a thick Scottish accent that belied his quintessential appearance.

"Mr. Douglas?" Jessica asked him.

"Aye, that's right," the man replied. "Jessica Newman, is it?"

"Yes, it's nice to put a face to the solicitor."

Mr. Douglas laughed, which added an even higher pitch to his Highland tone. "True, it is. Please call me William, though. Welcome to Mackinnon Manor."

Jessica knew none of them felt very welcome.

"Have you had a look around the house yet?" William inquired.

"We only got off the plane in Aberdeen a few hours ago and then we drove here," David told him. "I'm David Newman, Jess' husband, and this is our son, Alex."

William shook David's hand, but Alex just scowled at the Scotsman.

"Nice to meet you, Mr. Newman," William replied. "Was the flight from Heathrow reasonable?"

"It was long," Alex chimed in.

William chuckled and walked past them towards the house, briefcase in hand. Thunder grumbled above them again.

"You'll have to get used to our weather here pretty quickly," William said as he climbed the stairs. The Newmans followed reluctantly. The solicitor fumbled around in his briefcase as he continued talking. "This is actually considered our "dry" season, but when you live near a mountain range as wide as the

Grampians, you tend to get rain and fog all year round."

"Well, we'd better not stay outdoors for very long then," Jessica said.

"Aye, true again, Mrs. Newman," William said as he finally retrieved the keys to the house.

Jessica's stomach quivered when the solicitor put the brass key in the lock and turned it. A plethora of emotions and memories of a man she'd tried to forget were about to come rushing to the surface.

The hinges let out a long, creaking sigh as the door opened and about a decade of dust and naphthalene fumes struck their senses. The grey light of the morning scarcely touched the manor's interior, yet Jessica could not help but be captivated by the rich, lacquered oak walls and floors.

The vestibule floor was accented by a tapestry of tartan, emblazoned with what Jessica presumed was the Mackinnon family crest. A hallstand, built of matching oak, was the resting place for a walking cane and a well-worn fedora hat, the first direct link to Jessica's father. She recalled him wearing the same hat to church when she was a little girl, and it sent a chill through her spine.

Pushing the memory down, Jessica turned to the small banister on the wall opposite. She stared at the ornaments set upon it: a crucifix, empty spectacles case and two framed photographs—one of her father kissing the ringed hand of Pope John Paul II, and the other a picture of Jessica as a smiling young schoolgirl, a few years before her mother's death. The latter confused Jessica even more.

"This house was built in the eighteen-fifties," William told them. "The Mackinnon family was quite well-to-do in their day, I'm told. They were one of the largest cattle farming families in the area. I believe that Mr. Mackinnon was the only descendant to become a man of charity."

"Really?" David said, with a raised eyebrow. "The black sheep, was he?"

"David, don't," Jessica scolded him.

"Well," William continued. "Your father did his best to take care of the inside of the house, but obviously the exterior suffered for it. There are four bedrooms on the top floor and the dining, living rooms and study are down here. I believe Mr. Mackinnon slept in the master bedroom, but spent most of his time in the study."

"Is that where they found his body?" Alex asked.

"Alex! Please!" Jessica chastised him.

William sighed, but carried on. "Feel free to look around the house. I imagine we'll have to discuss your plans at some stage. Do you intend to put it on the market?"

"I don't know yet," Jessica replied. "I'm still trying to get used to the idea my father left me all this."

"I understand," William said, as he placed his briefcase on a coffee table.

"Do you know much about my father's time here?" Jessica asked, dreading his response.

"All I know is that he kept himself fairly busy helping the less fortunate here in Aviemore."

"The less fortunate?" David inquired.

"Yes, the homeless. Mr. Mackinnon helped prepare meals to give to the poor, mostly elderly people, but there were a lot of young ones as well," William explained.

Jessica found it hard to believe, her father being generous and kind. The Douglas Mackinnon she remembered could only be described as a monster. That was more than twenty-five years ago. Perhaps he'd changed, maybe even redeemed himself? Jessica was willing to consider any possibility to salvage something good from her past.

"Do you know the name of the place where he helped out?" Jessica pressed further.

"William smiled. "Aye, I do. It was at the old church in town, Saint Stephen's."

"I thought you said your father was expelled from the church all those years ago," David said.

"I did, and he was," Jessica told him, a look of surprise on her own face.

"Well, all I can tell you is that in Aviemore, no one is guilty of anything they've done in the past. You can start afresh here," William said.

"That sounds a bit idealistic," David retorted.

"It does. The folk here take people as they come."

Jessica looked around the room again, her mind full of pre-conceived notions and judgments. The skills she'd acquired when she was studying to become a child counsellor told her that judging someone by their actions was not the true way to get to know a person. She'd never put those skills into practice because her own troubled childhood kept her from fulfilling her future.

"Mr. Douglas?"

"Yes, Mrs. Newman?"

"Do you think you could show me where Saint Stephen's Church is? I'd really like to speak to some of the people there who knew my father."

"Jess," David said gently.

"Of course," William replied. "If you don't mind, can it wait until tomorrow? I've a mountain of paperwork back at the office."

"That's fine. I'd really appreciate your help. I'd also like to see where my father is buried, if that's possible."

"That won't be a problem." William grabbed his briefcase and the house keys. "Now, if you think you've seen enough of the house, I'll have to be locking the place up and heading back into town."

Jessica took the keys from his hand. "Do you mind if we hold onto these for a while?"

David frowned. "Jess, what're you up to?"

She turned to him, smirking. "What? I'm thinking we could stay the night."

"Are you sure? You weren't certain you wanted to come here in the first place. You were scared out of your wits on the plane over here."

Jessica glanced around the house again. "Yes, but now that I'm here it doesn't look that bad. Besides, we have to check the place out if we're going to sell it. We have to see how much work we need to put into it."

"You're not serious," Alex complained. "You said we were going to stay in a motel."

"Well, I've changed my mind, Alex," Jessica told him.

"You said we'd be here one night and then we'd fly back home," Alex continued, on the verge of an adolescent tantrum.

"I'm sorry, Alex, but I'm not ready to go home just yet."

David searched his wife's eyes for a hint of emotion, but she looked cool, calm and collected. Like always. He held her hand and smiled.

"Okay, one night," he said.

Jessica kissed him. Alex groaned.

"It's not proper procedure," William pointed out. "Legally, the house is in your name. As long as you take care not to damage anything, you can stay."

"We won't." Jessica assured him.

Minutes later they watched William drive away. Jessica jangled the keys in her hand and noticed a new wave of showers rolling in from the mountains. The heavy drops thudded on the roof sheeting and echoed within the manor's spacious interior like a thousand drums beating. David reached for Jessica, held her around the waist and kissed the back of her neck.

"You sure about this?" he asked.

"Definitely."

"Look, I'm glad you're taking such a big step, but I want to make sure you're not setting yourself up for a fall."

She turned and wrapped her arms around his neck and fingered his hair.

"My father's dead, David. He can't do me any more damage," she mused. "Maybe spending some time in his home will help me discover who he became in the twenty-five years he was here. Maybe, once I find that out, I can move on."

David kissed her. "Okay, Jess, I'm with you one hundred percent. As long as you're sure."

"There's not a doubt in my mind."

Boston, Massachusetts, May 8th, 1984

"**C**an you tell me what happened to your Mommy tonight?" Jessica looked up at the policewoman through flooding tears.

She'd never seen a policewoman before, but she was surprised by how pretty she was. Her shiny gold name badge said her last name was Andrews.

"She's gone to Heaven," Jessica told Officer Andrews, hoping she answered the question correctly.

Officer Andrews smiled and Jessica saw her eyes sparkle. Jessica liked her uniform and there was a little box with a cord like a telephone's on her shoulder that spoke in different voices. Officer Andrews noticed Jessica looking at the box and with a touch, she made the voices go away. Jessica was reminded of the story in the New Testament when the Apostles spoke in tongues—*Glossolalia*, her father called it.

"Where's my Daddy?" Jessica asked.

"He's talking to some other police officers. We're hoping he can tell us what happened to your mom."

Jessica wiped the tears from her eyes. She was cold, tired and afraid. Her Mommy had gone to Heaven, but her face had told her she wasn't happy to go. This didn't make sense to Jessica, because her Daddy always told her you couldn't help but smile when you met God.

So why didn't Mommy smile?

From where she and Officer Andrews were sitting in Jessica's bedroom, Jessica heard other men talking down the hall, in her Mommy and Daddy's bedroom. Every so often Jessica saw a light flash from that direction, like a photoflash. Jessica wondered if the men were taking photographs of her Mommy's face, to show how she hadn't been smiling when she went to Heaven.

"You okay, sweetie?" Officer Andrews asked.

Jessica sniffed. "It's past my bedtime," she said. "Daddy never lets me stay up this late on a Saturday. It's church tomorrow."

"I know, I'm sorry," Officer Andrews replied, her voice croaky. "We're just waiting for your aunt to arrive to pick you up."

"My aunt?"

"Yes, Honey, your Aunty Kay. You remember her?"

Jessica tried to remember all her aunts. She thought Aunty Kay had wavy blonde hair and a tiny, heart-shaped mole on her left cheek. When she laughed it sounded like it was coming out of her nose. Was she Daddy's sister or Mommy's? Jessica wasn't really sure. She rarely saw any relatives, unless they went to Church or Prayer Group.

"I'm not sure," Jessica said finally.

"She's your Mommy's sister. She lives in Lowell. She's much closer than your grandparents in Springfield, so we asked her to come and get you. She should be here soon, okay?"

Officer Andrews' smile put Jessica at ease. "Okay," she said. "You're a nice police lady."

Officer Andrews smiled back, but her lips were shaking. Jessica thought she saw tears in her eyes. The officer reached out to Jessica and tucked a loose strand of hair behind her ear.

"Thank you, sweetie," she replied. The policewoman glanced around Jessica's bedroom, as if she didn't want to look at her anymore. "You've got a nice bedroom. Mine wasn't this nice when I was a little girl."

Jessica considered her room; there was the large, wooden four-poster bed, with a crucifix on the wall above it, a little bookshelf desk stacked with one book, a *Good News Bible* her father had given to her as a present for her fifth birthday almost five years ago, and a tall wardrobe with a selection of Sunday dresses. The only other object was a framed photograph of Jessica and her parents, outside the Church on the wall near the door. She would have liked to have more, but as Daddy always told her, "The meek shall inherit the Earth."

"It's okay," Jessica said. "I'd like to paint it pink, but Daddy says pink is for little girls who don't know God."

Officer Andrews raised her eyebrows. "Is that what your Daddy thinks?"

Jessica nodded.

"What about your mommy, what did she think about pink?" the policewoman asked.

"Not much," Jessica replied with a shrug. "She stopped thinking a long time ago." She paused and bit her lip. "She stopped being Mommy a long time ago."

"What do you mean, sweetie?"

Jessica glanced at the floor, her voice barely audible. "Mommy used to smile a lot and laugh a lot, but then one day she became mean and kept trying to hurt herself. Daddy says she had the Devil in her."

"Did you believe that?" Officer Andrews asked.

"I don't know," she replied, looking across at the crucifix. "How could the Devil come into my daddy's house? He's a clergyman."

There was a long silence between them and Jessica stared out into the hall. She counted four more flashes from her parent's room, but then they stopped altogether. The men had stopped talking, too.

"Is there anything you want to tell me about what happened tonight, Jessica?" Officer Andrews asked; the question seemed very important to her.

Jessica was about to answer, but the sight of two men pushing a bed with wheels from her parents' room silenced her. On top of the bed was a long black bag, like a sleeping bag you'd take camping. The zipper along the length of the bag was slightly open and inside Jessica saw her mommy's strange face. She squealed. Officer Andrews turned to see it too and she ran to zip it closed. Jessica saw her look very angrily at the two men.

"Jesus Christ, show a bit of respect," Officer Andrews yelled at them. "Her kid's in there."

The men apologized and hurriedly wheeled the bed down the hall and carried it down the stairs. Officer Andrews ran back to be by Jessica's side.

"Are you okay, sweetie?" She held Jessica's hands. "I'm sorry you had to see that."

Jessica looked into the policewoman's eyes, shook her head and tsked.

"You said the Lord's name in vain, shame on you!"

Part Two

Once the Newmans had the place to themselves, Scotland's trademark weather soaked Mackinnon Manor almost to its foundations for three hours, as if the house needed to be cleansed.

As the rain fell, Jessica busied herself by preparing to settle down for the night, unpacking and making beds. She rummaged through old cupboards in the upstairs hall, while David surveyed the spouting. Alex chose to sit on the porch, looking as miserable as the rain.

Jessica found three thick woolen blankets in the hall cupboard. On her way to make the beds in the second and third bedrooms, she came to the door to the master bedroom, the place where her father had slept and dreamt and thought for twenty-five years.

The urge to open the door proved irresistible.

Jessica tried four brass keys from the set William had given her before the lock turned. The scent of naphthalene was even stronger than in the study, as if its inhabitant knew he would never return to it and secured it for good. Perhaps it wasn't her father's bedroom at all.

The four-poster, queen-sized bed certainly looked inviting enough, but it hadn't been disturbed. Neither had the heavy curtains which blocked even the slightest hint of light. Goosebumps flushed the bare skin of Jessica's arms and she tried to rub them warm; she felt the room was even colder than outside.

She took a few steps further into the room and studied every nook and cranny. The walls were plastered with intricately detailed floral wallpaper, faded with age, most likely the original. There was an old Bible on the dresser, an antique bureau drawer in one corner and a large two-door wardrobe in another. The only other piece of furniture was an ornate roll-top writing desk. Jessica ran her finger over the small, well-worn brass lock on its front and wondered what secrets it held inside.

A quick scan of the key ring told Jessica the key for the desk was to be found elsewhere. Resigned to the fact, she turned her attention back to the Bible on the dresser. She opened it at a random page and found the text saturated with almost illegible markings and writings. Whole passages were crossed out, while others were written over with vulgarities. Could her father have written such things?

Jessica scanned for the title of the book she'd opened to. *The*

Book of Job. She was familiar with the Bible; she was a deacon's daughter, after all, and if nothing else, her father had imposed upon her from a young age the purpose to read and understand the Good Word. That knowledge would never fade.

She was troubled by the words that were scratched over the text of one particular passage:

The Lord asked him, "What have you been doing?"

Satan answered, "I have been walking here and there, roaming around the earth."

The crude handwritten words virtually spilled out over the passage in a scrawling rage: "killing, raping, fucking, biting, cutting, ripping, tearing…"

The vile words flowed on and on, each one worse than the last. The words seeped into Jessica's head and the room around her became heavy, almost suffocating. Jessica swore she saw the vines on the wallpaper wither and die, but when she looked again, they remained unchanged. She quickly tossed the Bible away onto the bed, as if she'd held a venomous snake, and her confusion subsided. She couldn't wrench the image of her father scribbling all over the pages from her thoughts. Could he have truly been the monster he was made out to be?

"Jess, are you up here?" David called out, suddenly appearing in the doorway. His smile faded when he saw the tears on his wife's cheeks. He went to her and held her. "What's the matter?"

She wiped the tears away; seemingly unaware they were even there. She didn't want David to know about the Bible or the horrible graffiti throughout its pages.

"Yeah, I'm okay," she said, half-smiling. "I think I'm just a little emotional, that"s all."

"Are you sure you want to stay here? It's not too late to find a motel."

"No, it's okay, really." Jessica took his hand and led him out of the fearful room, carrying the blankets. She didn't want to go back in there ever again. Yet, she still couldn't quench her thirst for the truth about her father. Quickly, she closed the door and locked it.

"You okay, baby?" David asked again.

Her husband had that same look on his face: the one of caring concern he always wore when Jessica struggled with her emotions. He'd had the same look when they'd first met in the college laundromat and in the hospital, when she'd tried to take too many pills. He'd pulled her out of the dark then and he always would.

Jessica pushed her tears down. "Yeah, you go down and see what we're going to do about dinner. I'll be down in just a sec."

She watched David descend the stairs, leaving her alone with the depraved words in the Bible slowly burning into her memory.

Jessica feared she'd made a grave mistake.

Alex couldn't sleep.

The house was too vacant, too old and dark. He'd never admit it to his parents, but he could feel there was something not right with Mackinnon Manor.

As Alex rolled over in the ridiculously hard bed for the eighth time, he contemplated leaving his room and heading up the hall to check on his parents, just for the sake of seeing if they too couldn't sleep. He thought better of it and instead reached for his I-Pod on the bedside table.

He switched on the device and felt the soft white hue of its screen on his face. "Decode" by Paramore resounded in his ears and for a moment, he wished he'd packed his portable DVD player; at least he could have watched a movie while being forced to spend the night in his grandfather's old dump.

Alex couldn't understand why his mother wanted to visit the home of the man who'd killed her mother. If he'd had his way, he would have burned it to the ground already, erasing all the bad memories in a cloud of smoke and flame. But he was only a kid; he had to do what he was told. God, he hated being told what to do, which rules to follow, who not to believe in. Sometimes he wanted to reset all the rules and start again.

He'd never forget the first time he destroyed something with fire. The power was indescribable, the raw energy infectious.

It was last summer, during the school camp at the Blackstone River National Park. Alex wanted to go home as soon as he arrived. The moronic jock-heads teased him for days on end. Then it hit him. All it would take was one little spark and his worries would be over. That one spark became a brush fire and there was no choice but for the class and all the teachers to evacuate.

He'd never seen such fear in their eyes. Alex would savor it for the rest of his days.

Paramore's song ended abruptly, mid-chorus. Alex frowned; he'd charged the I-Pod only a few hours ago, but it was drained again. Groaning, he searched in the dark for the charger, but the soft white hue returned to its screen. When Alex looked, there was no music to be heard, no album artwork, only two black words.

"Help me."

Alex looked around the bedroom, uncertain. Then he ran his thumb over the I-Pod's central button to try and clear the screen. The two words remained. He tried to turn the I-Pod off, but the screen was frozen by the two words. Fear crawled in Alex's gut when the words suddenly blinked off and on, like Morse code.

Alex hesitated, but then spoke, "Who is this?"

He felt so stupid talking to a machine, but inexplicably, the screen replied with new words.

"Please Help Me. I'm In The Basement."

Alex swallowed. His mind raced with fear and confusion. Was there something wrong with his I-Pod? Was he imagining things? He found his mouth seeking answers, almost on a subconscious level.

"Who is this?" he said again.

The screen flashed another response. "Ewan."

"How are you talking to me through my I-Pod?" Another flash.

"It doesn't matter. Please, you have to help me!"

"How can I help you? You're not real," Alex said.

"Yes, I am. I'm in the basement. Please hurry. He's coming!" Then the message was gone, the screen was black again and the conversation was over. Alex felt his heart jack-hammering away in his chest and the palms of his hands were so slick with sweat, he almost dropped the I-Pod. He didn't know what happened, but somehow it felt very real.

Alex looked toward the bedroom door; outside was the hall, at the end of the hall was the staircase down to the study, off the study was the kitchen and in that room was the door to the basement. Even though he'd never wanted to set foot in Mackinnon Manor, that didn't mean he wasn't interested in taking a look around to see if there were any treasures he could pocket.

So, what should he do? Should he heed the pleas of this "Ewan", or discount the whole strange experience as jetlag and try to go back to sleep? Before he could decide, a piercing yell burst through Alex's earphones and he almost jumped out of his skin. A distinct voice, male and sounding in horrible agony, was calling for Alex's help. The plea was repeated on the I-Pod's screen.

Alex dropped everything and ran out the door. He screamed for his parents, but the scream from the I-Pod was even louder. Alex pounded on the door to the room where his parents were sleeping, but it was as if they couldn't hear him.

There was no mistaking that the scream was coming from someone in the basement, a person in absolute agony and in fear of his life. Alex wanted to go to them, but he was frozen in terror. Why couldn't his parents hear the scream? Why couldn't they hear their own son?

"Alex! He's gonna kill me!" the voice exclaimed from the ground floor.

Alex slinked down the staircase towards the kitchen. Other noises mingled with the screams, muffled thuds, bangs and a disturbing hiss. Under the horrifying crescendo of sounds was another voice, calm and monotone. To Alex, it almost sounded like someone chanting.

"Alex!"

Alex ran into the kitchen and grabbed a large knife from the drawer. He glanced at the basement door, took a deep breath and ran at it headlong, bearing his shoulder forward and bracing for the impact. Before he reached it, the door opened of its own accord. Alex felt his feet give way underneath him. He tumbled and rolled downwards, hard wood slamming into his back and knees in rapid succession. Abruptly, he hit the basement floor face first.

"Alex!"

Alex looked up and there, in the center of the room was a boy, a young man about Alex's age, tied to a chair. His face was contorted in pain and fear, his half-naked body drenched in sweat. The boy was looking straight into Alex's eyes.

"Please help me!" the boy begged him.

Alex lay on the floor, unwilling to move. His indecision was unfortunate for the boy. As Alex stared, something incredibly hot but invisible touched the boy's chest, just above his left nipple. The skin flared red and popped and sizzled for a second and then, a second later, burned itself black.

The boy roared in pain.

"He's gonna kill me! Alex, stop him, please!"

There was nothing to stop. The only people in the room were Alex and this boy, who was being tortured before his very eyes.

Alex wouldn't move. He wanted to call out to his mother, but he knew she wouldn't come.

Alex began to cry in helplessness and strangely, the boy forgot his pain. Alex was even more afraid of the hatred and murder he saw in the boy's eyes.

"If you don't stop him, Alex, then I'll tell him about your fire fetish!" he threatened.

Then, in a flash of black, the boy and the basement were gone. Alex found himself back in his bed. His I-Pod was dutifully playing Paramore again. The curtains were drawn and rain danced across the roof.

As Alex's heart rate slowly thudded down, he realized there was no need to be scared. There hadn't been any screaming. There had never been any boy being tortured in the basement.

It had all been a bad dream.

The previous night's rain looked to have cleared by the time William Douglas arrived at Mackinnon Manor to take Jessica into Aviemore town.

As William drove, Jessica engaged in idle chat with him and occasionally watched the rolling green hills of the Grampian Mountains blur by. Despite feeling rested, she still wanted to be distracted from the emotional turmoil she'd experienced in her father's bedroom the day before. Jetlag must have affected her body even more than the trauma.

Her mind was a different matter; she couldn't stop thinking about her father's Bible. William sensed her anxiety.

"Did you sleep all right last night, Mrs. Newman?" he asked.

"Yes, surprisingly, and please, call me Jess. I'm amazed how quickly I went off to sleep. We were all so tired; Alex was still sleeping when you arrived."

"Children seem to have so much energy, but still spend half their lives in bed." William replied, with a smirk. "Have you had a closer look at your father's house?"

Jessica cringed. She knew William was motivated to sell the Mackinnon Manor, but his incessant queries only reminded her of her father's secrets.

"I did. Structurally it's in fairly good shape for its age, but it certainly needs a lick of paint and David says the spouting needs a bit of work."

"Your father must have tried hard to care for the house, probably as much as he cared about the people of Saint Stephen's Church," William said. "I think the people there will have a lot of good things to say about him."

Jessica looked back out the window again; dark clouds were rolling in once more.

"Yes, it will be interesting to hear," Jessica replied.

William could tell Jessica's thoughts were a world away. There was an awkward silence as he turned his four-wheel-drive onto Grampian Road, the main road into Aviemore town. The green hills began to shift and change, giving way to cattle pastures.

"I hope you don't mind me saying so, Jessica," William said. "People can change, even the really bad ones. I can't pretend to know what it was like being a child and living through what happened to your mother, but although people can never forget, they can still forgive and be forgiven."

Jessica turned and smiled. "Yes, I know that. It's just…hard to forgive someone who betrayed you."

"Aye, it is." William said. "It is still within our power nonetheless."

"Don't take this the wrong way, but you sound like a priest."

"I suppose I do. Saint Stephen's has had a good effect on me since I first came here. It's my church."

Jessica frowned, curious. "Then you must have met my father."

"I only met him a few times. I've only been here a little over a year. I moved from Glasgow to start my own practice. I'm not a local yet."

"What was he like?" Jessica implored.

William steered left and Jessica saw historic buildings, delicatessens, butcher shops and cafes, all rolled together. Camera-cradling tourists surrounded an old railway station, with architecture that would have been more at home in Berlin. She felt comforted by Aviemore's quaintness.

"He was…quiet," William finally said, rather uncomfortably. "But he was hard-working. Look, Jessica, I don't mean to be rude, but I think it's best if I leave the descriptions to the people who were closer to him, if you don't mind?"

"Of course, I didn't mean to pry," Jessica replied, curious as to why William was reluctant to elaborate.

"Not to worry. Ah, here we are, Saint Stephen's Church." William pulled his four-wheel-drive in to park outside the church.

Jessica climbed out to take in its majesty and feel the brisk North Sea air on her face. To Jessica, the church looked more like a cathedral on a slightly smaller scale. Constructed of sandstone blocks, its center point was a high steeple, which seemed to keep a vigil on the town and its people, who were busy walking and talking.

Jessica turned around to observe the street behind her. It appeared the town had been built around the old church. The building looked centuries old, but it had weathered the Scottish elements. William led her towards the entrance. As she followed him, she caught sight of an ornate stained-glass window mosaic depicting a man on his knees, head turned skyward, while two men raised large stones above his head—Saint Stephen, the martyr.

Inside, the church was considerably more modern and a hive of activity. The pews had been pushed aside to make way for tables and chairs. People milled about, showing a whole range of art and craft. Jessica had to remind herself that churches were not meant to only open on Sundays. The church felt homely to Jessica, somewhat dissimilar to the parish her father was in charge of running when she was a child.

As they studied the busy church, a young man, dressed in a neat, short-sleeved checked shirt and tan pants, suddenly approached them from the crowd. A pair of horn-rimmed spectacles framed his pleasant face; he resembled a young Bill Gates. He smiled widely and took William's hand.

"Hello William, it's good to see you," he said. "What are you doing here? I didn't think you were into patchwork and quilting."

"Oh, no, Father Osmond, I'm not the knitting type," William chuckled. "I'm showing Mrs. Newman around the town."

"Oh," the priest replied, turning to consider Jessica. He offered her his hand and she shook it. "Mrs. Newman, is it? Are you new to town?"

"No, just visiting actually," she said.

"You're American?" Father Osmond observed.

"Jessica is Doug Mackinnon's daughter," William revealed.

"Truly?" Father Osmond shook Jessica's hand a little more enthusiastically, which brought a smile to her face. "Oh, what a privilege it is to have you here." Then his expression became more downcast. "Please accept my deepest sympathies for the loss of your father."

"Thank you," Jessica said. "I understand my father volunteered here. I was hoping to…learn a bit more about him."

"Jessica hasn't seen or heard from her father since…her mother passed away," William said.

Father Osmond frowned. "Oh, that"s such a shame. He did speak of you on occasion. I got the strong impression he really missed you."

The priest's statement took Jessica aback. She always assumed her father abandoned her, but now she was even more desperate to garner the truth about him from Father Osmond.

"Do you have time to talk now, Father?" Jessica asked.

"Not right at this moment, I'm afraid," he told her. "I have to keep an eye on the craft event here, but it should finish up in about an hour. Perhaps you could come back and meet me here, later this afternoon."

They agreed. William, however, had to leave Jessica and attend his work at the office. They said their goodbyes and Jessica walked the streets of Aviemore, sightseeing like any other tourist. Strangely, she didn't feel comfortable; it was like she was an invader. She was so confused about her father and she found it difficult to accept everyone's recollection of him as a caring soul. She hoped Father Osmond would finally be able to put her mind at ease.

Before William drove away, he pointed Jessica in the direction of Aviemore Cemetery. It was a few blocks from Saint Stephen's; the steeple's giant shadow almost pointing Jessica in its direction.

Apprehension gripped Jessica's chest. What was worse: meeting your long-lost father, or standing over your long-lost father's grave? Steeling herself, she wandered inside the grounds and gazed at all the headstones and monuments jutting out of the lush green grass. A woman's voice suddenly brought her back to the living world.

"Can I help you, Miss?" the woman said.

"Ah, yes, hello," Jessica replied. "I was wondering if you could help me. I'm trying to find the grave of...Douglas Mackinnon."

The woman smiled. "Oh, you're...a relative?" Jessica nodded. "His daughter."

"I can show you where he's buried if you'd like. My name is Donna."

She led Jessica to a plot on the western side of the cemetery. She looked about seventy years old, but she moved about the cemetery quickly, like it was home. In the front row was Deacon Douglas MacKinnon's headstone, a modest, rectangular shape engraved with his name and dates of birth and death. For a long while, Jessica studied the headstone and played with her necklace, a simple heart-shaped locket that belonged to her mother. It was the only thing she'd been allowed to salvage from her body.

"There were a lot of people at his funeral," the woman said. "People from the church and even some of the poor homeless folk he helped feed."

Jessica turned to the woman. "Did you know him?"

She shook her head. "Not really. I used to see him around town sometimes, standing next to the meal van, talking to the homeless. He seemed genuinely interested in their problems."

"Did you go to Saint Stephen's?"

"Yes, I did."

"Did my father ever help during the service...as a deacon?"

Donna shook her head. "No, but I remember he preached scripture and gave me some passages to pray with when my sister was dying of cancer. He preached to a lot of people, especially the homeless."

Jessica thought of him preaching, as he had with her mother the night she died.

"I'm sorry to keep asking you questions, but could you tell me what scripture he preached from?"

Donna frowned. "Oh, I can't remember, love, it was so long ago."

Jessica held up her hands. "I'm sorry," she said, trying to appease her. "I guess I'm trying to find out what sort of a minister he was. He used to read me passages when I was a little girl and I'm curious to see if it was the same with everyone else."

Donna nodded in understanding. "He knew the Word and he knew the right way to help us seek guidance or redemption. He was a good cleric."

Jessica smiled and thanked Donna for her help and candor, but she hadn't divulged any real information. She left the cemetery feeling empty, robbed of any hope. She'd walked for several blocks, when the aroma of coffee attracted her to a café.

While she was at the coffee shop, David rang her on her mobile phone. She told him about her visit to the cemetery and how she felt, as if she'd been left with inanimate objects as memories: her mother's locket, and her father's headstone and house.

"We could get a good price if we sold the Manor," he told her.

"We'll see," she replied. "How's Alex?"

"Still asleep."

"Really? I thought he'd be out of bed by now."

"No, he must have been exhausted last night. He hasn't set foot out of his room."

"Well, can you wake him soon? It's past ten o'clock and I don't want him sleeping all day."

"How did things go at the church?"

Jessica sighed. She didn't want David to think she'd wasted her time, but she needed to confide in him: he was her touchstone. "I met a priest there that knew Dad. I'm going to meet him later."

"Did he have much to say about your dad?"

"Much the same as the solicitor, Dad was a very nice and helpful minister."

"Maybe it's the truth?"

"Maybe, but that's not the way I remember him."

"Well, the priests he worked with have known him the longest, Jess. Don't be afraid to get them to tell you the truth, okay?"

"Okay."

They ended the call and Jessica waited at the café for another ten minutes before she walked the few blocks back to Saint Stephen's. She found Father Osmond waiting outside for her. He appeared agitated and the priest didn't return her casual smile.

"Thank you for coming back, Mrs. Newman," he said. "I think it would be better if we talked inside."

"Is something wrong?"

"Please, if you would come inside."

Jessica followed Father Osmond into the church feeling unsettled by his sudden change of mood. The church's interior looked more like it should, with the rows of pews facing the altar, but the space was flooded with shadows. Father Osmond sat on the front row pew and encouraged Jessica to sit next to him.

"I'm sorry for all this secrecy, Mrs. Newman, but this is a private matter after all."

"What do you have to tell me?"

Father Osmond was pensive. "There are many things I must tell you...about your father."

"What things?" Jessica demanded. "What's going on? I can't

get a straight answer out of anyone in this town about who he was."

Father Osmond rested his hand on Jessica's. "Your father was a good man, but he was suffering."

"Yes, it was called guilt."

The priest glanced briefly at the crucifix hanging on the wall above the altar, before turning back to look Jessica in the eye. "Your father was a brilliant man, but he couldn't let go of his past and I feel it ultimately led him to take his own life. He came to Saint Stephen's not long after he left America. I didn't meet him until about ten years ago, after I left the seminary. Up until he died last year, I got to know him and witness his work with the homeless and the youths. He was very determined to help them get their lives back on track."

Jessica frowned in frustration. "I know all this. William told me some of it, but now you're saying there was something else?"

"Douglas used to talk…about your mother's death, whenever he could. We never prompted him. It was in the past and we don't dredge up the past. He was obsessed with telling us about it. He wanted us to understand he still believed he'd done the right thing."

Jessica felt sick. She didn't want to hear anymore, but Father Osmond persisted.

"Please, Mrs. Newman. I know this hurts, but if I don't tell you, I feel you will never be able to live the rest of your life peacefully."

"All I want is the truth."

The young priest sighed and he suddenly looked well beyond his years. "Your father was still convinced, even till his dying day, your mother was possessed by demons when she died. Worse still, he felt many people were possessed by demons.

"The church recognizes demonic possession, but there has to be considerable proof. You, of all people, should know, in the past, many psychological conditions have been misinterpreted as demonic possession. This didn't matter to Douglas; he believed everyone was susceptible. We tried to get him to seek counselling, but he wouldn't listen. Sometimes, I swear, it was almost as if he was one person when he was working with the homeless and another when he was with us."

Jessica stood and looked to the front doors of the church, desperate to leave.

"I want to thank you for your time, Father," she said, her voice shaking a little. "I'm going back, so I have to leave it there. I need to go back to the Manor and prepare to return to the States."

Father Osmond sighed again. Jessica saw, despite releasing the burden he'd held in for many years, he still felt lost.

"Of course," he finally said. "I'm sorry if I have offended you. Your father was a very troubled man. He was alone in his misery. I don't know if I've helped you, but I felt it was important to tell you what I knew."

"I appreciate that, Father. I don't know what to think of it, but you got to know my father a lot more than I ever could have. It seems he hadn't changed at all; perhaps he'd even gotten worse by coming here. It makes me sad to think he still manipulated people and lied."

Father Osmond stood and placed a gentle hand on Jessica's shoulder. "I hope you find peace someday, Mrs. Newman. I hope you can forgive him."

Jessica didn't reply; she walked down the aisle, determined to leave any feelings she had for her father behind in the church. She would sell Mackinnon Manor and go home, forget the man who'd died there and get on with her life.

May 9th, 1984, Boston, MS

Aunty Kay was crying and yelling when she drove Jessica to the police station, two days after her mother went to Heaven.

Since she picked Jessica up from her home in the city, Aunt Kay had been nothing but angry and sad. Sad about her sister dying and angry with Deacon MacKinnon. Jessica couldn't understand how you could be sad about one thing and angry with another. She knew you could be angry and sad; perhaps Aunty Kay was being angry and sad, but in an adult way.

Either way, Jessica was confused. It was only a few nights ago that Aunt Kay drove Jessica out of the city to her home in Lowell and now they were driving back.

"Why are we going back to Boston?" Jessica asked from the back seat of Aunt Kay's tiny car.

"The police want to talk to you, Jess." Aunt Kay replied as she tried to change lanes and wipe her nose at the same time.

"About Mommy?"

Aunt Kay blinked and Jessica watched as fresh tears slid down her cheeks. Aunt Kay was very emotional, even more so than Jessica's mom, before she got the Devil in her.

"Yes, Jess, they want to talk to you about your mom. They're trying to figure out how she died." Suddenly Aunt Kay became angry again. "Although it's pretty obvious how she died, that hypocrite she married is the one responsible."

Jessica frowned. "Do you mean Daddy?"

Aunt Kay turned her head sharply, as if she only just realized her niece was in the car. She wiped her eyes and tossed the hand tissue on the passenger seat.

"Oh, I'm sorry, Jess," she said, blubbering. "You're too young to understand what's going on. You probably don't even know why the police are involved." Aunt Kay unstuck her tangled blonde hair from her tear-soaked cheeks.

"Do they think Daddy hurt Mommy?" Jessica asked.

Aunt Kay flashed the little girl a look of concern. "Don't you?"

"Daddy would never hurt Mommy. He's a deacon."

Aunt Kay's face suddenly flashed red, as if she was about to say something mean to her. Instead, she turned the wheel and drove along a long, dirty-looking street flanked by lines of police cars. Jessica had never seen a police car before. Eventually Aunt Kay brought her car to a stop at a sign that said *Boston Police South Boston District*. Standing on the sidewalk was a familiar face, Officer Andrews and another dark-skinned lady. Aunt Kay helped Jessica out of the car and led her to the two women.

"Hi, Jessica," Officer Andrews said. "How are you doing, sweetie?"

"I'm okay. I miss home, but Aunty Kay is looking after me."

Officer Andrews smiled at her aunt. "That's good to hear," she said. "Can I introduce you to a friend of mine?" The policewoman indicated the dark-skinned lady, who came forward and shook

Jessica's hand gently. "This is Diana," Officer Andrews continued. "She works for the city—in Children's Services. She's going to go with you when you speak to the detectives."

"De-tec-tives?" Jessica said, uncertain.

"Yes, hon, they're police officers like me. They'd like to speak to you about what happened to your mom."

"They'd really like your help, Jessica," Diana added with a smile. "Do you think you could talk to them for us?"

"Will Aunty Kay come too?"

Aunt Kay put a hand on Jessica's shoulder. "I can't be in the room, Jess, but I'll be right next door listening—okay? Now you go with the nice ladies."

Officer Andrews and Diana led Jessica down the halls of the police station to a small room with no windows. They brought her a soda, but she didn't drink it—because Daddy called it "poison for the mind". Jessica sat silent, praying three Hail Mary's to stay calm.

Eventually two men entered the room; they were tall, but one was a bit fat with big hands. The hair on his top lip looked like a mouse was sleeping there. The other man was much younger and had no hair on his lip. The two men sat opposite Jessica; the fat one put a box on the table with buttons on it. He pressed the red one and looked Jessica straight in the eye.

"Hi, Jessica," the fat man said with a deep voice. "My name is Des Hartley. I'm a police detective and I'd like to talk to you about what happened at your house on Tuesday night. Would that be okay?"

Jessica looked toward Officer Andrews, who nodded. "It's okay, sweetie, Mr. Hartley's a nice man and he just wants to ask you some questions."

Jessica turned to the younger man and pointed at him. "Can he ask me the questions?"

Mr. Hartley's mouth opened wide and he stared at the younger man. "Uh, sure, Jessica, if that's what you want."

Officer Andrews and Diana chuckled and Jessica smiled. She turned to the younger man. "What's your name?"

"Michael. Detective Michael Dalton."

Jessica gasped. "Michael! Like the Archangel!"

Mr. Dalton laughed. "Yes, sweetheart, like the Archangel."

"Okay, you can ask me questions."

Mr. Dalton straightened his tie and slicked back his black hair with his hand. "Okay, Jessica, now if you feel uncomfortable at any stage, you just say 'stop.' Okay?"

Jessica nodded.

"Do you remember what you had for dinner on Tuesday night?" Mr. Dalton asked.

"Um, roast beef and potatoes."

"Was it good?"

"Yeah. Daddy always makes good roast beef."

Mr. Dalton frowned. "Your mommy didn't make it?"

"No, she stopped cooking a long time ago. Daddy said she couldn't be trusted in the kitchen."

"How so, Jessica?"

"Because of the knives," Jessica told him. "Daddy said she might hurt herself, or us if she had a knife." Jessica suddenly cringed as she realized everyone was staring at her.

"Are you okay, Jessica?" Mr. Dalton said.

"Mommy had a knife."

"When was this?"

"On Tuesday night—she came into my room with it."

Now everyone in the room looked scared. Mr. Dalton leaned closer. "It's okay Jessica, you're safe here. You can tell us."

"She tried to cut my hair." Jessica showed them the shorter section of her hair. "Daddy caught her and...he took her back to his bedroom. He was really angry with her."

Mr. Dalton swallowed and looked toward Mr. Hartley, who gave him a nod.

"Okay, Jessica, you're doing very well," Mr. Dalton told her. "Now, do you know what happened in your daddy's room?"

Jessica closed her eyes and thought really hard. "I couldn't see, but I heard Daddy praying. Mommy was shouting at him... She was cussing at him. Then Daddy started praying really loud, a prayer he hadn't taught me. Then Mommy screamed."

She opened her eyes. Officer Andrews was crying and Mr.

Hartley and Mr. Dalton were sharing worried looks. Diana took a hold of Jessica's hand and squeezed. Mr. Dalton smiled, but it wasn't a happy smile.

"Jessica, what do you think happened to your mom?"

Jessica blinked at the question, but she wasn't sure she had the answer. "Mommy used to do strange things. One time she went outside in the snow naked. We found her in the city in the water fountain. Daddy used to say Mommy had the Devil in her and I think when she cut my hair, Daddy tried to get him out."

Mr. Dalton spoke slowly. "So do you think…your daddy hurt your mommy?"

"Mr. Dalton?"

"Yes, Jessica?"

"I'd like to stop now."

Part Three

Jessica got in the first taxi she saw and ordered the driver to take her back to the Manor.

As much as she liked William Douglas, she didn't want to waste any more time in Aviemore, or impose upon the solicitor any further. She wanted the entire time she'd been in Scotland to be forgotten: a distant memory like all the rest she'd locked away for twenty-five years, only to foolishly release them again. Fighting back tears, she retrieved her mobile phone to call David and tell him to pack, when it suddenly rang in her hand.

It was David, and his voice was thick with desperation. "Alex is gone," he gasped. "I can't find him anywhere!"

"What do you mean 'he's gone'?" Jessica's heart raced with worry.

"I went in to check on him about half an hour ago and the bed was empty. His bed is still made. I've looked for him everywhere."

"Why didn't you call me?" she snapped, causing the taxi driver to flash her a look of concern. Jessica's growing fear only succeeded in heightening her husband's.

"I thought he'd gone off for a walk to sulk or something, but I doubt he'd wander off somewhere he's not familiar with."

"Have you tried his mobile?"

"Yes, it keeps ringing! God, do we need to call the cops?"

"Keep trying his phone. He"s got to be around there somewhere."

"We haven't seen him since last night!"

"Please, David, we both need to stay calm. I'm almost back at the Manor, so wait for me and then we'll look for him together."

Alex was truly gone.

Jessica and David searched the house together from top to bottom, under beds and in cupboards. Jessica even unlocked the master bedroom and searched its furnishings, but it was fruitless; their son wasn't in the house. David scoured the grounds, running wildly through the long grass calling Alex's name, but there was no reply.

Jessica twirled a strand of hair around her finger nervously as she selected her son's cell number from the phonebook in her own phone. It rang and rang, the incessant unanswered trill mocking her. She ended the call and immediately redialed, but the line simply rang out a second time.

She paced the hallway and rechecked cupboards she'd previously searched. Through a bedroom window, she watched David jog in a ragged line through the grounds in a similar state of panic. Jessica pledged that when she found her son, she would ground him for the rest of his life.

As she redialed for a second time, she descended the stairs into the foyer, the phone pressed to her right ear. As she passed the kitchen, a ringing suddenly echoed in her left ear. She stopped and listened intently; it was the ring from another phone!

When the call rang out, Jessica redialed immediately and tried to pinpoint its location inside the house. She stood at the entrance to the kitchen and tried to block out any incidental sounds. The ringing was dull, as if it was trying to pass through something solid, like a wall.

Her gaze fell on the closed door off the kitchen, the entrance to the basement. She called for David, ran to the basement door and tried to turn the knob. It was locked. She heard her husband enter the kitchen with frantic footsteps and heavy panting. Jessica turned and saw he was sucking in air, and sprouting heavy beads of sweat from his forehead.

"Why did you scream?" he gasped.

Jessica pointed at the basement door. "Alex's phone...I think it's down there. Listen."

She hit redial and David's eyes widened with realization when he heard the other phone's reply. But Jessica wasn't smiling.

"What?" David said.

"The door's locked," she told him.

"Do you have the key?"

"I don't know which key opens it," Jessica said, frantically fumbling with the clattering key ring in her free hand. "I haven't had the need to go down into the basement."

David squared his shoulders. "Get out of the way!"

Jessica complied, as David went into a full run and slammed the heel of his right shoe into the door. The door budged under the force, but it didn't give. David kicked again and the wood around the lock cracked and released, slamming the door inward into the wall.

The basement stairs vanished into a dense darkness and Jessica felt a slight breeze of cold air on her face. Instinct screamed at her not to go down the stairs, but David took a step closer into the doorway.

"Alex?" he cried into the darkness. Nothing.

"Alex, are you down there?" Jessica called.

There was only the dark looking back at them. David put his foot on the top step. Jessica gripped his arm and when David turned, he was startled by the fear in his wife's eyes.

"Don't!" she begged him.

"Alex might be down there!" David reasoned. "He could be hurt."

Dark memories of twenty-five years ago bled into Jessica's mind; she was sitting in that hallway in Boston, listening to her mother's screams. The same fear was in her heart again.

"We should call the police," she told David.

"I'm going down there," he replied, desperate. "Are you coming?"

Before Jessica could respond, David proceeded down the steps, the darkness devouring him as if he'd dived into an oil slick. Jessica was left alone to stare at the darkness.

"David?" she called.

Jessica moved down the stairs one at a time. With each successive footstep, she was lost deeper into the darkness. She waved her hands in front of her, reaching for anything to connect her back to the real world. She prayed she would touch David. She prayed her son was safe, anywhere else other than down here.

"David? Alex?" she called again, her voice echoless in the black basement.

"Here," David finally replied. Jessica knew by the jerkiness of his voice that he was shaking.

She followed the sound and gradually the darkness receded to shadow and then a mottled grey light, like the sun struggling through fog. Jessica saw David staring into it. She too looked into it, eager to determine its source.

Jessica stood next to David and he grabbed her hand and squeezed it, a physical warning to his wife. Ever since they'd met, she'd known David to be composed and calm, but for the first time she could feel a terrible tremble of fear in his grip. Suddenly she knew why.

A boy was tied up in the center of the room. He was naked, with thick ropes around his wrists, ankles and neck, bonds so tight they had stripped his white skin red raw. The marks paled in comparison to the others that riddled his body: bruises, cuts, scratches, welts and burns—a sickening montage of violence.

The boy looked lost in the glow, like he wasn't really there at all. Jessica's maternal instinct kicked in; she wanted to rush to him and cut his bonds and mend his wounds, but the little girl inside told her to run and hide.

Slowly, the boy lifted his head and smiled at them, a string of bloody saliva sliding from his bottom lip to the floor.

"Alex isn't here right now," the boy said. His voice, distinctly Scottish, resonated around them.

"Who are you?" David asked, trembling. "Where is my son?"

The boy smiled even wider and his blackened eye sockets flushed maroon with bruised blood. "I've seen him around," he replied.

"Do you know where he is?" David asked again.

"I'll tell you if you untie me."

David stood firm, while Jessica's mind raced with fear and doubt; they had no idea who they were dealing with and she kept thinking the boy could have tied himself up.

"I'm not going to do that," David said.

The boy suddenly began to sob and shake his head uncontrollably. He stamped his feet and screamed. Then he begged them with bloodshot eyes.

"He's going to come back soon!"

"Who's going to come back?" Jessica suddenly asked, anxious. She looked toward David, who shared her fear. They needed to stay strong if they were to find their son.

"The bastard who did this to me!" the boy screamed.

Jessica turned around to look behind her at the staircase. She wanted to be sure no one was there. Reassured, she turned her attention back to the boy who was now as terrified as she was.

"Who hurt you?" Jessica cried. "Did someone bring you here?" "Yes! The old bastard brought me here. He did this to me and he's coming back!"

David stepped a little closer and he felt a tug on his hand. He felt Jessica squeeze his fingers, a sign she was begging him not to go.

"It's okay, Jess," he told her. "I just want to talk to the boy."

Jessica reluctantly released her grip and David stepped even closer. He held up his hands in a placatory gesture to show the boy he wasn't going to hurt him.

"What's your name?" he asked.

The boy smiled coyly. David saw some of his teeth were missing. The raw gums gave the impression they'd been recently knocked out—or forcibly pulled out. David tried to sympathize with him, but he was yet to decide if it was safe to approach the boy.

"Ewan," the boy replied, glancing wide-eyed from her to David.

"Okay, Ewan," David said. "My name is David Newman and this is my wife, Jessica. Alex is our son." Ewan nodded in acknowledgement.

"You obviously sound Scottish. Where are you from?" David said.

"You're obviously American," Ewan replied, somewhat sternly. After a moment's pause, he answered. "I'm from Aviemore."

David frowned. "Do you know where you are?"

"Yeah, this is the old bastard's house. He brought me here, said he was going to give me a place to sleep and some work. Then as soon as I went to bed, he dragged me down here and beat the shite out of me!"

David turned and shared a knowing look with his wife, whose eyes were wide with dark realization.

"When did this happen, Ewan?" David asked.

Ewan dropped his head and Jessica saw he was trying to recall. "Last night," he finally said. "He drove me back here yesterday. He gave me some food and sent me to bed."

"Ewan, we were here last night. We've never seen you before, or any old man."

Ewan looked genuinely confused and even more afraid. He looked from David to Jessica and to the door at the top of the basement stairs. Tears rolled down his cheeks.

"You're lying!" he said.

"We've only been here two days. This is Jessica's father's house."

Ewan shook his head again and pulled on his ropes. He was suddenly like a caged animal.

"No! That bastard brought me back here last night!"

"Okay, okay, Ewan," David said, trying to soothe him. "Who is this man? Can you tell me more about him? Can you tell me his name?"

Jessica's scream suddenly cracked the air; she was as wild-eyed as Ewan.

"Tell us what you've done with our son!"

Ewan opened his lips to reply, but then his gaze was caught by something on the stairs behind them. Jessica turned to look, but there was only the soft afternoon sunlight radiating down from the kitchen that she could see.

Then Ewan screamed, a shriek of sheer horror, high-pitched and wailing.

"He's here! No! You fucking stay away from me!"

David and Jessica looked at the stairs again, but there was still nothing to see; there were only the three of them in the room. Successive cracking sounds made them turn back to Ewan, who was being struck across the face repeatedly by a succession of invisible blows. The boy's blood flew across the air, onto David's shirt and face. Jessica screamed.

As the shock struck their senses, the dull light bled away to black. Ewan, and the violence being inflicted upon him, vanished.

Jessica felt sick; she'd witnessed the unbelievable. Neither she nor David wanted to admit what they'd seen, but there was no denying it. Jessica sought an explanation from within; she needed to know where her son was, she wanted to know who or what Ewan was and why he was in her father's home.

"That was a ghost, wasn't it?" David muttered, breaking the cold silence of the basement.

"I...think so," Jessica replied.

"Do you think it will come back?"

Jessica stared at the spot where Ewan the ghost had sat, screaming in agony. "God, I hope not."

"He said he knew where Alex was," David reminded her.

Jessica turned to him. "Can you really believe that?"

"Jesus, Jess, can we believe anything anymore? I mean, what the hell is going on here in this house? Who was that kid, and what was torturing him? What did he mean about your father bringing him here? Your father's dead."

Jessica pushed her hair back with her hands; the back of her neck was sweaty with fear despite the icy temperature of the basement. She grabbed her hair and twisted it into a make-shift ponytail. Feeling a little calmer, she started to think.

"I don't know, David, but maybe we should call the police."

"What do you think they'll be able to do?"

Suddenly a howling wind drifted into the room, a wind that carried a voice, as low as a whisper. The voice escaped into the air like steam. Jessica and David stood as still as statues, listening intently, captivated by the sound. The noise swirled around them, almost in stereo, and Jessica could literally feel it touching her ears and skin. Neither of them dared to speak.

Before their eyes, the sound took shape and form, wisps of crimson smoke twirling and coalescing in the dark. The gaseous ribbons smudged on the air, thickened and metamorphosed a second time. The smoke took on the shape of a body, a man. The figure stepped and gestured in slow motion, moving from one side of the room to the center. The shape was determined, it had a task to perform, but Jessica and David had no inkling what it was.

The smoky silhouette formed words, but the syllables were distant. Jessica heard the words, but they were too deep and too fast to comprehend. It was when she was struggling to translate the strange language that a piercing scream overwhelmed everything. Ewan's naked, trembling form reappeared in the exact same place as before, but this time he couldn't see Jessica or David. His eyes were wide and fixed on the smoke man. "Please, you have to let me go!" Ewan begged.

The translucent man ignored Ewan, muttering and gathering invisible objects in his hands.

Jessica tried hard to recognize the man, but the vision faded in and out, like a lighthouse beacon. The shape suddenly stepped before Ewan and pushed something into the boy's arm. Ewan screamed as his blood spurted to the floor.

Jessica and David were watching Ewan being tortured, but this time his torturer was visible, or at least partly visible. Jessica wondered whether she was watching the past or the present. Inexplicably, mental footage of her mother's face, frozen in death broke through; it was only for a split second, but she felt a shock of emotion, as though it had only been yesterday.

Ewan kept screaming as the shape shifted around him, pulling his teeth, slashing and cutting him, in an almost rehearsed rhythm. Jessica glimpsed the shape of the hands and saw they were always full of some object, a weapon in one hand and something that looked like a book in the other.

A Bible.

"Stop it!" It was David, yelling at the wraith. "Stop! Leave him alone!"

"David, don't!" Jessica said hoarsely; she wanted them to remain hidden.

The smoke creature stopped dead in its tracks and stared in their direction. It drifted and bent in the air like an ethereal snake as it approached them. It saw them. It saw them as if for the first time.

"Oh God—its face!" Jessica screamed.

Spirals of acrid smoke twisted in and out of the orifices of the face; a human face, comprised entirely of soul fog. A face Jessica knew all too well, even twenty-five years on.

The face of Douglas Mackinnon.

The face roared with a cry that shook the basement walls. Jessica screamed back, turned and ran for the stairs, with David on her heels, calling to her as the grotesque figure chose to pursue them.

David's sudden, sharp pain-induced scream made Jessica stop. She turned to find the smoke man enveloping her husband's legs, dragging him back down the stairs. She wanted to help David, but terror and her need to escape pushed her out the door.

The afternoon sun struck her eyes hard, and Jessica had never been so grateful. She slammed the door closed and sat up against it on the floor, determined to keep it shut. A moment later Jessica realized she'd heard herself crying and screaming out for help, but she knew her only hope was in the basement, at the mercy of the unholy beast.

Boston, MS, June 10, 1984

Jessica had never met a Bishop before.

He was tall and dressed in black with a purple sash around his waist. He had long, gangly arms and a tiny round cap on his head. What Jessica noticed the most about him was his eyes:; how pale they were. Jessica saw herself in his eyes. That made it easier to look at him.

Jessica's grandparents brought her to the Cathedral to meet with the Bishop. Jessica didn't like the Cathedral because there were too many shadows, and churches were supposed to be bright, golden places. As she sat in the front pew beside the Bishop, she wondered why her father never brought her to the church before.

"I'd like to thank you for coming to meet with me, Jessica," the Bishop said with a slight smile. "I wanted to meet the brave little girl everyone's been talking about."

Jessica looked at the Bishop for a moment before turning away to consider the enormous stained-glass window of the Christ Child holding a lamb above the altar. She knew what "brave" meant—brave was Jesus dying on the cross.

"How are you feeling, Jessica?" the Bishop said.

"Okay."

The Bishop forced a smile. "I know that things…have been hard for you, but I want you to know you shouldn't feel what happened to your mother is your fault."

Jessica turned back to the Bishop. "The police say it's Daddy's fault."

"Yes," the Bishop nodded, as if he could hardly bear the thought.

"They say Daddy…killed…Mommy. But killing is a sin—a mortal sin."

"Yes, killing is a sin—a grave sin, Jessica. It's one of the Ten Commandments."

Jessica felt a tear roll down her cheek, only to fall onto the palm of her hand. It was wet, and warm, but of no comfort.

"Daddy would never kill anyone, especially not Mommy. He loved her. He loved me."

The Bishop held Jessica's hands; his skin was cold. "This is a lot for you to understand, Jessica," he said. "The police are certain your father took your mother's life. They have charged him with her murder."

Jessica hung her head low and nodded. "The Devil…" she muttered.

"What did you say, child?"

"The Devil…" she turned her moistened gaze to the Bishop.

"Daddy said Mommy had the Devil in her… What if he tried to get him out?"

The Bishop shook his head. "No, Jessica, your mother was very sick."

"You believe in the Devil, don't you, Bishop?" Jessica was sobbing now. "My Daddy did! He only wanted to free Mommy!"

"Hush, Jessica." The Bishop took her in his arms and held her as her cries echoed inside the darkened Cathedral.

"Daddy would never lie," she said, her face buried in the Bishop's shoulder. "He said lying was a sin, too."

The Bishop cradled her face in his hands. "Your father was a very confused man, Jessica. He should have helped your mother, not hindered her. She needed medical attention."

"Daddy said God would help us," she told him. "Daddy said God would help him find a way to free Mommy. Why didn't God help Daddy?"

The Bishop felt tears pricking at his own eyes. The poor, precious little girl had lost everything, and was close to losing her faith. He tried to think of the words to say. How could he tell a little girl that sometimes God didn't help? He glanced down the aisle to see Jessica's grandparents, seated at the back, fighting off their own sadness. He'd asked to speak to Jessica alone, but the girl was strong of spirit. He saw the irony in the fact that her teacher was also a murderer. He stood and, holding Jessica's hand, walked her to the altar.

"You are a very special young girl, Jessica," he said. "You are very brave and very wise for your age. I think that in a way, this is how God is helping you to get through this." He stared at the Christ Child's fragmented visage. "Don't turn your back on God, Jessica. It might seem that right now he has turned His back on you, but know he will always love you."

"What about Daddy…does he love me too?"

The Bishop felt his stomach clench. "He did what he thought was right, Jessica. But he was wrong. He made the wrong choice for you and your mother."

"So, I shouldn't love him anymore?"

The Bishop crouched down and gazed into her almost crystalline eyes. "You should always love, Jessica. Remember what Jesus taught us: 'Love one another as I have loved you.' He also taught us to forgive."

"I don't know if I can forgive Daddy."

"You have to try. If you can't forgive, you will carry it for the rest of your life."

"Would you forgive him?"

The Bishop swayed and rested on his knees. Jessica's questions pained him. "If he sought forgiveness...yes."

Jessica studied the stained-glass window for a few moments, the afternoon sunlight casting her face in a crescendo of colors. The Bishop imagined her imbued with holy light. Then, she turned to him once more.

"If I forgave Daddy, would he get into Heaven when he died?"

"As I said, your father would have to seek forgiveness from God. Only God can judge him in the end."

Jessica turned back to the window. "I wonder if Daddy will smile when he sees Heaven, or will he cry?"

"I'm sorry?"

"Mommy wasn't smiling when she went to Heaven. I don't understand why. Why wouldn't you smile when you saw Heaven?"

The Bishop knew why, but he had to give Jessica hope. She needed hope more than truth right now.

"She was...taken from life too soon."

"Would she be smiling now?"

"I think so...yes."

The Bishop began to lead her down the aisle and he signaled to her grandparents. Little Jessica suddenly took the Bishop's hand and squeezed it.

"I know I'll smile when I get to Heaven, I'll see Mommy again." The Bishop laughed softly at her innocence. "Of course you will, child."

"I know I'll never see Daddy again, he'll be in Hell."

With that she ran to her grandparents, who greeted her with open arms. The Bishop was shocked by her final words and her comprehension of damnation, but deep down he knew she was right.

Part Four

Douglas Mackinnon was dead.

For all her life, it was the only truth Jessica had left to hold on to, but now she lost that grip. There was no earthly reason for what she had seen. First Ewan, and now the vengeful soul of her father, their ghosts tormenting her and her family.

Jessica knew in her heart why he was here. She knew what he was doing; continuing the foul work he'd begun in the real world all those years ago. He hadn't escaped to Scotland to start anew, he had only found another home for his torturous acts. Ewan was only his next victim.

She wiped the tears from her eyes and thought of David and Alex being terrorized by the specter. She had to go to them, to save them, but how could she when she'd never been able to save herself? Twenty-five years of grief left her powerless to handle life, let alone the supernatural forces in the basement. She needed David, her knight in shining armor. She grimaced at the irony of how the tables were turned on her.

Even through the veritable safety of the door, Jessica still saw her father's face in the back of her mind. He, this so-called man of God, was a killer after all. He killed his wife and now he threatened to kill his daughter and all she loved.

The silence coming from the basement only fueled her imagination. She saw smoke creeping across the floor, swirling around David, ready to seep into his lungs and eat him from the inside out. Then it would slink its way to Alex and flay the skin from his bones. Him, her dreadful father, was putting the sickening pictures into her head.

He must have lured Alex into the basement, she thought; it must have been his plan all along: kill himself and bring Jessica out of her life and back into the dark to torture her all over again. There was no denying the truth anymore, her father was evil and he had to be stopped.

But how?

She felt the solid door on her back and she turned to stare at the well-worn brass knob. All she had to do was turn it and venture back into the dark—confront her father one last time.

Fear crawled into her throat and fresh tears flowed. She dropped her face into her hands and cried, her body trembling with sorrow and pain. What had she done to deserve this life; to see her mother fall apart, to watch her murdered, to know her father was the killer? Why have twenty-five years of relative peace only to have it all torn asunder once more?

Stop crying, Jessica told herself. *Get up and face it. Do something for yourself for once in your pathetic life. This is it, your chance to fight back. Take your father on face-to-face.*

Jessica scrambled to her feet and reached for the doorknob. Where had that authoritative voice originated? She never spoke to herself that way before, she'd always retreated and cowered behind stronger people, like David. Now that she had no shield, she had to create her own.

She gripped the icy doorknob and turned it, revealing the gaping mouth of her living nightmare, the nightmare of her past come back to haunt her. She took a deep breath and stepped into its maw. Once she was gone, the door closed. A faint whisper rose in the air to turn the door's lock, trapping her inside.

The basement was colder and staler than before. The smell of blood and smoke was so strong, it almost crawled down into Jessica's throat to claw at her stomach.

Her eyes managed to find David in the dark. He was face down, unconscious, but thankfully still alive. Jessica ran a gentle hand through his hair and bent to kiss his cheek. It seemed her father wasn't interested in him—at least not yet. She swallowed hard and clenched her jaw; she wasn't going to relent, not this time. She wasn't a little girl crying in the hallway anymore.

Jessica blinked the tears from her eyes and thought of her father, his blasphemous words and his frozen hands around her mother's throat. She smiled as a picture of him slumped in his chair in the study slipped into her thoughts; she wished she'd been there to see that. Seeing his ghost would have to suffice.

The mirage of Ewan, strapped to his chair, suddenly appeared before Jessica, like a light being switched on. His ghostly form was thinner and much bloodier than before, but Jessica wasn't interested in him.

"Go away!" she spat.

"Help me, Jessica, please!" Ewan sobbed, his tears running a line through the blood caked upon his cheeks.

"I can't help you, Ewan."

Ewan's features shifted to anger. "So, you're going to let him torture me over and over? You fucking bitch!"

Jessica ignored him and searched the room for any sign of the smoky trails of her father's malevolent spirit. There was only darkness.

"Where is he?" Jessica asked.

"Not here, thank Christ! I don't want him back here anytime soon."

"Come out," Jessica cried at the dark. "Come out and face me!"

"Shut up, bitch!" Ewan railed, trying to free himself again from bonds that he could never break.

"It's me...Jessica," she cried into the dark. "You know you want to speak to me. I know you have my son!"

"Please, stop it," Ewan muttered.

"Shut up," Jessica shouted, silencing him.

Then smoke began to seep through the cracks in the concrete wall behind Ewan. The boy yelped when the tendrils caressed his shoulders, as if they were savoring the blood on his skin. The shadow of Douglas Mackinnon stepped through the fog and considered his daughter with a slanted look.

He stared at her for some minutes over his half-moon spectacles, which appeared permanently fused with the flesh of his nose. A dull spark burned in his eyes like coal and his skin was flushed with hot blood in steady, flowing ripples of red. He was a much different ghost to Ewan—fiercer, sharper, and ravenous.

Jessica stared back at him, adamant she wouldn't avert her gaze. This was a standoff twenty-five years in the making. She watched as a sneer crossed the former priest's mouth, then he ran a hand through his widow's peak, like he was preening himself. Jessica could feel his arrogance and she retaliated in kind.

"Where is my son, you bastard?!"

Douglas' smile widened. "Is that how you greet your daddy after all this time?"

Jessica tightened her fists. "Tell me where he is!"

"I don't have him," Douglas shrugged.

"Bullshit!"

The deacon's wraith chuckled heartily. "Oh, such language! You wouldn't have gotten away with it when you were a little girl, no sir."

"Where is Alex?"

Douglas' candor was wiped clean, and in an instant he was upon Jessica, his hand clamped like a vice around her throat. His strength was impossible and his smoke enveloped her with the scent of sulphur and ash.

"Don't you talk to me like that, you little whore! Don't talk to me like your mother did."

Jessica tried to draw breath, but she couldn't even swallow. Douglas sneered again. "You're just like her, you know. It's scary, actually, how much alike you two are inside as well as out. Maybe you should have been killed as well?"

Jessica saw the darkness closing in as black sparks appeared behind her eyes. Then Douglas released her and she fell to the ground, sputtering and gasping for precious oxygen. Douglas floated back to Ewan and stroked the coagulated blood in the boy's hair.

"I haven't got time to reminisce, Jessica, my girl. Ewan and I have unfinished business."

Jessica pulled herself to her feet as Douglas reached into thin air and retrieved a pair of rusting pincers and waved them under Ewan's nose.

"Why are you doing this?" Jessica wheezed.

Douglas frowned at the interruption, his skin flushing redder in response.

"What?" he chided. "Are you still here? Answer me! What are you still doing here? You're dead!" Douglas let the pincers go and they floated in the air and followed him like a vicious familiar.

"Well," Douglas replied, almost chatty. "I suppose I could humor you a while longer."

Jessica knew she was conversing with the ghost of her father, the man she'd not seen for a quarter of a century. But even in life, she'd never known him to be so mischievous, so conniving.

"To be blunt," he continued, "I enjoy it. I always have, ever since the life was squeezed out of your mother. So, I thought to myself, why not keep doing what you do best?"

"Is that why you killed Mom?" Jessica said.

Douglas smiled and shook his head and began to chuckle. The deep cackle became a rolling guffaw, as if Jessica had told him the punch line to the funniest joke of all time. When he was done, he wiped a blood-tinged tear from his eye.

"What's so funny? Jessica cried, tears streamed down her face.

"Oh, Jess," Douglas said, his hand to his chest. "You've got me all wrong. I didn't kill your mom."

Jessica pointed at him. "Don't you lie to me. You admit it, you bastard! You tell the truth for once in your miserable life."

Douglas held up his hands in mock surrender. "I'm sorry to disappoint you, Jess. It wasn't me who killed her, it was your dad."

The thing that was Douglas Mackinnon wet its lips with an unnaturally long tongue and smiled as Jessica struggled to understand the revelation it had delivered.

"You're not taking this very well, are you, Jess?" Douglas said. Jessica blinked and looked from Douglas to Ewan, who was all too aware of the inside joke.

"You…you're not my father?" Jessica stuttered.

"Technically, no," Douglas replied. "This is his essence. I'm borrowing it for a while."

"Then, what…are you?" Jessica gulped.

"Your daddy was wrong on a lot of levels, Jess, but he was always on the mark when it came to one thing—your mother's state of mind."

Jessica tried to comprehend the apparition before her; the way her father's visage mocked her.

"She really was possessed," Jessica said.

Douglas slapped his knee gleefully. "Now you're getting it! Who do you think the demon was inside her?"

Jessica closed her eyes and fresh tears streamed down her face.

"You," she replied.

Douglas shot his arms out into the air, as if he were the ringmaster of some psycho circus. "Bingo! See, you're not so stupid after all. You see, your daddy followed the exorcism playbook to the letter; he extracted me from your dear old mom, but I had to find somewhere else to go when he strangled her. So, the logical thing for me to do was to jump into his bag of bones."

Jessica dropped to her knees and sobbed. Her father freed her mother after all, but in his misguided heroism to prevent his wife from being subjected to possession again, he killed her. His efforts, however, had proven unwise.

"So," Douglas continued, "I brought your daddy back here to the family home. For twenty years or more, I took him out on the town every once in a while, and we had a whole lot of fun with derelicts like Ewan here. No one ever shed a tear for the homeless, but your dad started to break through my defenses and mouthed off to his priest buddies about me. Luckily for me, they thought he was crazy.

"Then he went and decided to top himself. He thought that would free him and stop our fun. How wrong he was. I wouldn't let him get away that easily. Ever since that day I've haunted his soul and used it to keep up our good work."

Douglas drifted right up to Jessica's face and she felt the burn of his breath on her skin.

"Your daddy's a great torturer; look at how he worked on me!"

Jessica couldn't speak. She wanted to flee. She'd heard the truth and now she wanted no part of its madness. The dark forces within her father's home threatened to swallow her and she had to save herself and her family. She looked to Ewan. "Please, Ewan, where is Alex?"

Ewan's ghostly eyes flashed disdain. "How the fuck should I know?"

"Don't lie, you know where he is," Jessica retaliated. "You must have been the one who brought him down here."

Ewan looked from Jessica to Douglas, terror anew in his eyes. "Is that true?" Douglas asked, gripping Ewan by the hair.

"No!"

Douglas cracked a sardonic smile. "I know you're lying."

"All right. All right," Ewan squealed. "I know where he is."

"Good boy," Douglas said. "Don't feel bad. It's very inventive of you. You're trying to save yourself, but it's still very naughty. You will have to be punished."

Ewan trembled as Douglas plucked a Bowie knife from the fog. The boy stared at Jessica, pleading.

"Help me!"

"Give me my son!" Jessica shouted.

Ewan's anger resurfaced and his pleading eyes fell on Douglas. "If you let me go, you can have the boy!"

"No!" Jessica wailed, running forward to silence Ewan, but Douglas hissed at her to keep her distance and all she could do was comply.

"That's a very interesting proposition, Ewan my boy."

"No, please, don't!" Jessica was inconsolable and it was her turn to beg.

Ewan ignored her. "Will you let me go?" he said to Douglas.

"Where is the boy, then?" Douglas asked, almost salivating at the prospect of a new victim.

Ewan glanced past him to a hole in the wall, a drain covered by a metal grate. The rusted bars were closed tight over a space that looked from the outside to be not much wider than three feet square.

Jessica saw a tuft of Alex's dark hair and a streak of blood on his pale forehead. To her, he looked dead.

"Alex," she cried.

Douglas smiled and gripped Ewan's shoulder proudly.

"Oh, very good," he said, excited. "You may have redeemed yourself!"

"So, you will let me go?"

Douglas approached the grate and crouched to consider

Alex's motionless form. He reached in through the bars and ran a finger along the smooth surface of the boy's arm.

"What a blessing," he whispered. "A true descendant of Douglas Mackinnon for me to shape, educate and savor."

"Don't you touch him, you bastard," Jessica warned.

Douglas turned, his eyes afire. "Don't you talk to me like that. If it weren't for you, I would still be living the high life in your mother's perfect little soul." Then he turned back to Alex and with one effortless tense of his arm, he pried the grate free and tossed it aside. "Maybe I can start anew in a young Mackinnon body."

"You leave him alone!" Jessica screamed.

Ewan struggled to free himself from his chair.

"He's yours!" he exclaimed. "Now let me go."

"You're free," Douglas replied.

Ewan rejoiced, but then his expression became a cringe of pain. He jerked and writhed and Jessica watched in horror as smoky black blood poured from the boy's mouth and nose and eyes.

Douglas plunged his enormous knife into Ewan's back and greedily sliced and stabbed like a mad butcher. Then the demon-possessed spirit of Jessica's father reached his hands inside the boy's ethereal frame, digging like a hellhound through flesh, muscle and sinew until he found what he searched for.

Douglas pulled Ewan's spine free from its resting place, like he was unsheathing a sword. The boy's body fell empty to the ground and crumbled like bloody charcoal. Then Douglas held the spine above his mouth, the string of bones dangling over his tongue.

Jessica turned away when Douglas suddenly sprouted razor-sharp teeth and crunched them down on the vertebrae. It took the demon a few seconds to swallow each one, the sound of the crushing bites like gravel being turned to dust under a steamroller. When she found the will to turn back, she saw Douglas holding Ewan's skull in his hand.

"Now for the main course," he snarled.

Douglas lifted the skull to his lips and slurped and sucked as if he were eating an oyster. The bloody soul smoke inside Ewan's skull oozed out into the dead deacon's mouth. The contents were sucked dry and the cranium was left looking like it had aged a thousand years.

The demon deacon wiped his maw on his sleeve and smiled in satisfaction.

"More," he said, turning to Alex.

"No!" Jessica shrieked.

For the first time in twenty-five years, Jessica prayed to God, a silent recitation that, out of desperation, became a mantra. She prayed for forgiveness for her mother's failings, her father's sins and for herself. She prayed to God and all His heavenly hosts to give her a sign, an indication that her life hadn't simply been to suffer unending grief and torment. Jessica pictured her mother's face becoming a smile, her eyes turning to behold the Creator in all His impossible splendor.

Jessica opened her eyes and found her mother standing in the basement, a pool of inner light pushing back the shadows. She felt her mother's voice in her heart, like an embrace.

"Jessica," her mother said.

Jessica couldn't speak, mute with joy and disbelief. Her tears answered for her. Felicity Mackinnon, resembling an angel, glided across the darkened air to her.

"There's no need to fear, Jessica," Felicity said. "I'm here now." "Please, help me," Jessica pleaded. "Stay with me."

Felicity reached out and wiped away her daughter's tears. "So many tears you have shed, daughter. You are drowning in them. But no more." She turned to face Douglas' demon, who writhed with rage.

"You can't touch me, bitch!" he exclaimed. "You're nothing."

Felicity smiled. "That is true, I cannot touch you." She held out her hand to Jessica. "But my daughter…"

Jessica slid her hand into her mother's and warmth flowed through her skin, deeper and deeper, through flesh and bone and blood, until her heart pulsed with Felicity's golden light. Jessica felt alive, drawn out of the darkness that had overshadowed her since that awful day in 1984. Then her eyes were forced open.

Two golden swords of light sprung from the sockets, striking Douglas in the chest. The pure white light ate at the wraith's ribcage, growing, spreading and brightening. Douglas' screams cracked the basement walls, shaking bricks loose to fall on the ground. The white light from Jessica's eyes turned the red smoke of Douglas' body to ash and then to nothing. He was gone and all his darkness with it.

Jessica felt her body go limp and she collapsed to the ground. Her chest heaved and Felicity's soul passed out of her daughter into the empty basement. There was no demon, no Ewan, only Jessica, David and Alex, who started to rouse from unconsciousness.

"You're safe now," Felicity told them. "The demon is gone. Banished to Hell."

Jessica smiled at her mother. She wanted to run to hold her and never let her go again.

"Thank you," Jessica replied.

"Come," said her mother. "There is much more to show you."

Jessica, David and Alex suddenly found themselves standing inside Douglas Mackinnon's bedroom. As they all tried to fathom how, Felicity entered the room in a flash of sunlight. She moved to Douglas' writing desk and produced the key to unlock it.

The Newmans watched as she retrieved a bundle of envelopes and handed them to Jessica. There were hundreds of them, all addressed to her.

"These are from your father," Felicity said. "He wrote them during his lapses back to normality. He wasn't free from the demon long enough to pass them on to you. You need to read them."

Jessica stared at the spirit of her long-dead mother. "How… can you be here?"

"It was you, Jessica," Felicity said as she cupped her daughter's trembling fingers around the letters. "Your faith brought me here. You never truly lost it."

Jessica shuddered with sadness. "But…why?" she said. "Why

take so long to come back to me? Why did all this have to happen to me?"

Felicity pondered the letters in her daughter's hands and Jessica imagined her reading the words through the envelope.

Instinctively, Jessica cradled them. They were more precious than gold now.

"Do you remember what your father used to say? 'God tests us all?'"

"I remember."

"Satan tests us too, Jessica. Many times we fail, but sometimes we win. In the end it's our choices that matter. Your father chose to end my suffering, but in turn he brought that suffering upon himself...and you. Despite all that, my daughter, you've stood the test of time. Without you, we never would have been reunited."

Jessica turned to David and Alex, both still silenced by disbelief. "They helped me, too."

"Yes, they did," Felicity said, smiling widely. "You have two very brave men there. You look after them."

Felicity turned to leave, but Jessica caught her arm. "Wait. Don't leave. There's still so much more I want to know."

"You know the truth."

"Yes, but what about Dad, where is he?"

"He is being cared for."

"But...he killed you."

Felicity took her daughter's hand again. "Yes, but he saved me. That demon tormented me for years, your father many more. He sacrificed himself for me and you. Can't you see that?"

Jessica turned to her husband and son again and this time they were looking toward her. They saw the truth and were begging her with their eyes to see it too.

"You still...love him?" Jessica said to her mother.

"Of course. I always have and I always will. We'll see each other again. You need to start loving him again, too. Read the letters and you'll see the truth. He loves you. We both do. Goodbye sweetheart."

With that she was gone, like she'd never existed. Jessica and her family were left in the Mackinnon house, numbed by the mystery of all that had happened since they first walked through the front door.

Still, Jessica was drawn to the letters her mother left behind and she tore the top envelope open. It was dated June 24th 1985, Jessica's eleventh birthday:

> *Dear Jessica,*
>
> *I don't have a lot of time.*
>
> *I will try and write to you when I can muster the strength.*
>
> *I hope that one day you can understand what happened between your mother and I and why I had to free her.*
>
> *I hope even more that you can forgive me. I hope God can find it in His heart to forgive me and free me from this curse.*
>
> *I'm sorry and I love you.*
>
> *Dad*

"I command you, unclean spirit..!"

ABOUT THE AUTHOR

Two-time Bram Stoker Award® and multiple Australian Shadows Award nominee Greg Chapman is a horror author and artist based in Brisbane, Australia.

Greg is the author of several novels, novellas and short stories, including his award-nominated debut novel, Hollow House and collections, Vaudeville and Other Nightmares (Specul8 Publishing) and This Sublime Darkness and Other Dark Stories (Things in the Well Publications).

His works have been well-received by readers and critics alike, with many praising his ability to create gripping and atmospheric horror stories.

Chapman's writing is known for its vivid descriptions, strong characterisations, and intense emotions. He often explores themes of loss, grief, and trauma his work, using the horror genre to delve into the darkest aspects of the human psyche.

He is also a horror artist and his first graphic novel Witch Hunts: A Graphic History of the Burning Times, (McFarland & Company) written by authors Rocky Wood and Lisa Morton, won the Superior Achievement in a Graphic Novel category at the Bram Stoker Awards® in 2013.

He was also the President of the Australasian Horror Writers Association from 2017-2020.